Out of Nowhere

Out of Nowhere

S.C Karakaltsas

Karadie Publishing
Melbourne, Australia

National Library of Australia
Cataloguing-in-Publication Entry
Creator: Karakaltsas, S.C, author
Title: Out of Nowhere/S.C Karakaltsas
ISBN: 978-0-9945032-4-4 (paperback)
Subject: Fiction
Cover Artwork: Con Karakaltsas
Cover Design: Anthony Guadabascio (www.continue.com.au)

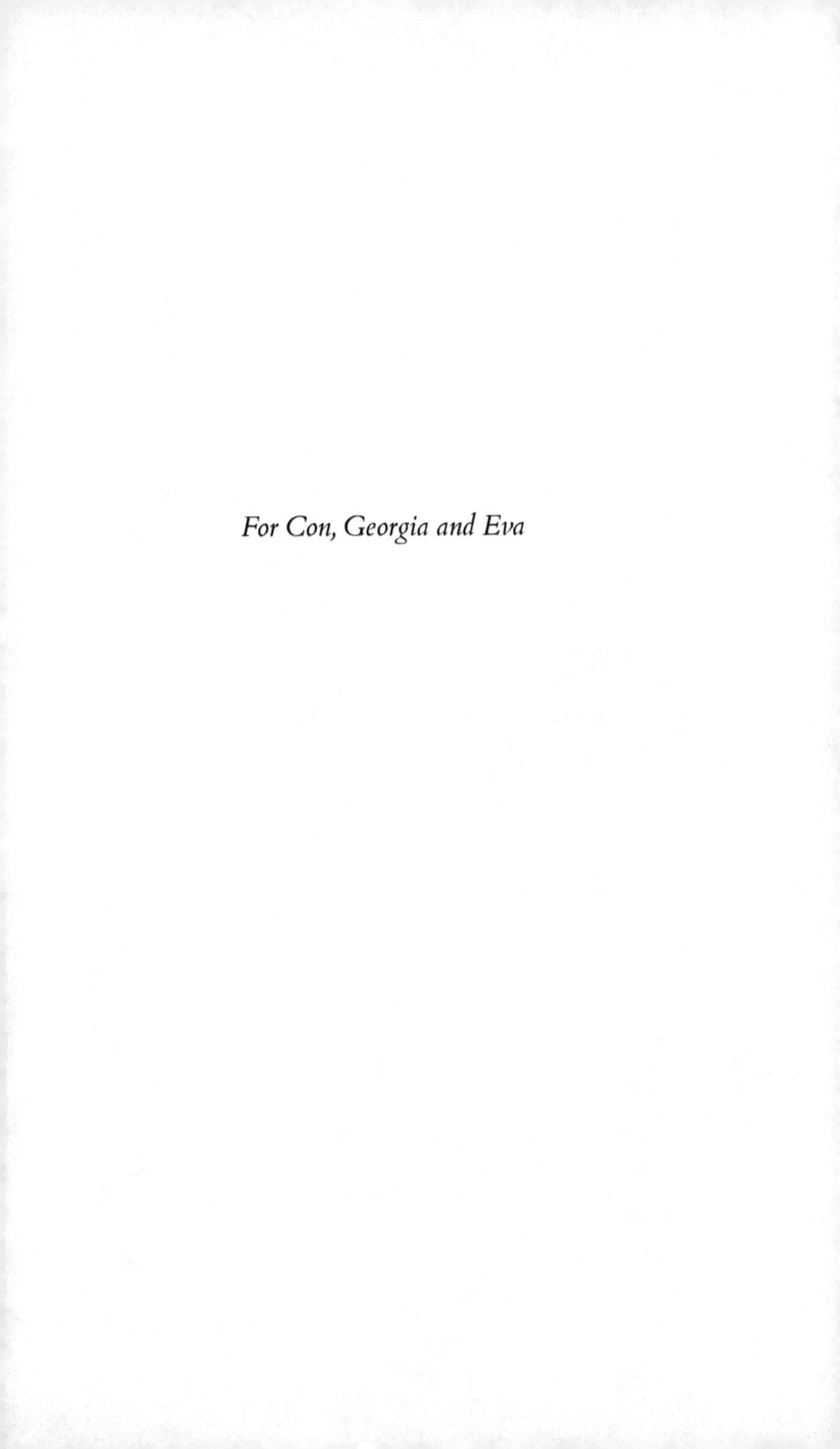

For Con, Georgia and Eva

Contents

ix

1. The River   1

2. Escape   12

3. When I Really, Truly Have To.   18

4. Nosy   24

5. Revenge   28

6. The Nut   40

7. The Black Satin Pants   54

8. It Was Only One Time   69

9. The Surprise   79

10. On The Side Of A Hill   86

11. The Holiday   95

12.	A Reason To Get Up	118
13.	I've Got News	136
14.	Out of Nowhere	157
15.	The Robbery	164
16.	Lucky	175
	Acknowledgements	185
	About the Author	187
	Other Books	188

1

The River

The sound of water entices me across a carpet of perfect lawn. It's not until I'm in the middle that I see the sign 'Keep off the Grass'. There's no-one around but I tiptoe – as if it would make a difference. Light spray settles on me from the fountain which splutters into the blue sky disturbing a brown mirror of water.

I walk the short distance along the river's path toward a collection of red striped umbrellas perched on a grassy hill. At the service window, I order breakfast, then find a table in a shady spot. The skinny latte soon arrives with its pretty leafed picture on the froth and it tastes good. Happy to be alone, I enjoy the cool breeze and take in the view of the river.

Relaxing into my chair, I savour my morning off, and avoid checking my emails. But I can't resist glancing at the Fitbit suctioned to my wrist. Five thousand steps, my heart rate is seventy and the day stretches ahead to easily allow me to reach my goal of ten thousand. Then, wrestling it off my wrist, I'm curiously relieved to be free of it.

Nearby, a workman in an orange vest yells something to his mate in matching gear. A rope of orange iridescent flags circles an area of lawn that holds the men's attention. In its centre, poles protrude from the ground. In front of one pole, a man in a long-sleeved white shirt and dark slacks talks to a third workman. I'm trying to figure out what's going on as I roll the coffee around my mouth before swallowing.

"But if anyone asks, tell them we're fine," a dark-haired woman pleads as she heads to a table in front of me. She rubs her arm and sits with her back to me. A shorter blonde woman, whose frown shows her worry, scrapes a chair along the wooden deck to sit opposite. They glance at a group of teenage girls in school uniform settling under a tall pink- barked gum tree. The girls write on folders nestled in their laps. Miss Dark Hair crosses her legs under the wooden chair. There's a small tattoo around one ankle and a large menacing bruise covering the other.

A flat boat pulls up and spits out its curious passengers and the dancing spray spurts even higher in greeting. Other people mill around, waiting to take their ride down the river.

"So sorry," a deep voice says, "the chef forgot your order. He's doing it now."

The waiter smiles with a look asking for forgiveness as he glances at my half-finished latte. "Can I get you another coffee? On the house?"

His eyes take in the map spread out in front of me. "Oh, no thanks. I'm fine."

"It shouldn't be too long," he says, watching the passengers coming up the rise toward the cafe. "The boat leaves on the hour if you wanted to know."

It's ten forty-five.

"Thanks, I might go later." But he's already disappeared and I give up the idea of making it in time for the next departure.

The crowd from the boat settle themselves at the vacant tables around me. An older couple are animated while talking excitedly in a language I don't understand.

The flat boat blows its whistle and pulls away, leaving a pelican prowling along the bank. A small child cries from somewhere behind me but I can't be bothered to turn my gaze away from the river.

The roar from a machine hauls me from my peace; maybe it's a whipper snipper. It's a relief when it stops.

"Here you go," the waiter says. He plonks a plate of poached eggs, tomato and avocado in front of me.

Before I can say thanks, he's gone.

"You've got to do something. If you don't, then I will," Miss Blondie says. "This can't go on." The long curls from her companion shake in response.

My latte is cold. Draining the glass, I wish I'd taken up the waiter's offer. Instead, I cut the sour dough toast and try to stop my plate from sliding across the table.

The roar starts again drowning everything else out. I tense. The two workmen are on either side of a large machine that looks to be drilling holes into the ground. The noise stops.

"Braydon ... Braydon, stop doing that. You'll get your pizza in a minute." A mother pulls in a massive pram with seats for three and expertly parks it next to me. She picks up a small girl in a pink dress and matching hair band, and sits her in a seat.

"No!" the father says. With his muscled tattoo-sleeved arms he picks up a bigger boy and puts him into a seat at the end of a table big enough for six. "You need to sit down first." He has a nice smile as he hands the boy iced tea – an odd choice for a child who looks about four. "C'mon Braydon, come here." The father picks up another child who must be Braydon and gives him a blue water bottle.

The waiter places lattes in front of the parents and a tray of food on the table. "Got your hands full today," he says, looking at the four children.

"Yeah, we have that every day. We hit the jackpot with triplets," the mother says wearily. But then she proudly smiles at her brood.

"At least you get it over and done with," the waiter laughs. "And I thought a three-year-old was a handful. How old are they?"

Suspending a delicate mound of toast piled with egg, tomato and avocado on my fork, I listen.

I miss the answer when the drill starts up again, but relish the taste of my food. More workers arrive and are doing something with the poles which seem to have wires hanging halfway down them. The drill stops and two workers ram a pole into the neat hole they've made.

"Harry, come and have a chip," the mother says. Harry is a replica of Braydon. He's standing too close to me and my half-eaten breakfast. His pudgy hands clutch dirt which he flings under my table barely missing my feet and white jeans. I'm relieved when they're all seated and the drill drowns out the family's strained banter.

A sweaty red-faced runner pounds past. The two women have left their empty glasses behind on the table and stand under the tree talking to the circle of teenage girls. They must be their teachers. Miss Dark Hair looks to be in charge. She points to the top of the tree and the long sleeve of her white shirt falls back. The girls look up, missing the cream bandage wrapped around her forearm, which she quickly drops back to her side.

The drill stops.

"Maddie, Mummy's cutting it for you. Pizza! Yum."

I wipe the last corner of toast around the plate for the remnants of egg yolk and slip it into my mouth. My phone beeps and I read the text asking me to be ready to do my presentation at two. It's eleven twenty. I can go on the boat and get back in time.

Maddie decides on a high-pitched squeal.

"It's hot darling. Just wait a minute."

The mother sings, "The wheels on the bus go round and round ..."

A drink bottle crashes to the ground and rolls dangerously close to me. Picking it up, I hand it to the father who smiles his thanks before turning his head sharply.

"Braydon ... No ... Come back!" The father bolts after his son who disappears behind me. The other coffee drinkers turn to watch.

"Harry, stay here," the mother demands holding onto Maddie and the other boy. But she's too late. "Harry!" she yells.

Meanwhile Braydon is running toward the workmen and the circle of orange flags.

"Braydon ... Stop ... Braydon. Come back here!"

the father yells. He doesn't realise Harry is right behind him. The mother is draining the last of her latte, daring the other two to move with unspoken threats.

The teenage girls and the teachers watch the chase but the workmen are too busy to notice. They're doing something with the poles. First with one and then another. It looks familiar. So familiar that I squint at them in disbelief. Is that what I think it is?

The father has caught Braydon and they're rolling on the ground. Harry has jumped on them and the three are laughing. But their laughter soon stops, as they too watch what the workers are doing. Like petals opening in slow motion, the poles turn into Hills Hoist clothes lines. I strap on my Fitbit and pick up my backpack from beneath the table. I want to get closer.

The school girls get up too leaving their books under the tree. More people have wandered over, when I reach the flagged ropes. There's another 'Keep off the Grass' sign. The clothes lines are going up one by one. The school girls are chattering while Miss Blondie talks to Mr White Shirt, the flagged rope separating them.

I listen.

"I heard about this artist."

"How did he think up something like this?"

"I should've brought my washing."

Laughter.

I count six perfect rows of four poles – eight have turned into clothes lines. I try to push the wheels on the bus song out of my head but it persists.

"They're always doing some sort of art installation here."

I follow Miss Blondie's glance to Miss Dark Hair who's guarding the books and bags under the gum tree. She's on the phone and pacing.

Another clothes line springs up and then another. I'm beginning to perspire and wish I'd brought a hat.

A siren squeals in the distance.

Harry and Braydon are standing next to their father, counting, one … two … three … four … five. The mother has the other two children but she struggles to push the pram over the grass toward them.

I look over at Miss Dark Hair. She's off the phone, but a tall muscular man in a singlet and baggy track pants is talking to her. He's side on to me but has something in his other hand. She looks angry but I'm too far away to hear.

More giggles from the schoolgirls. "But I don't get it. It's stupid if you ask me."

"It's better than class. Hey, I reckon the man in the white shirt is the artist talking to Miss."

"Let's get out of here. C'mon, no-one'll notice."

The girls chatter is behind me and I'm tempted to turn around so they know I've noticed, but I don't.

The drill starts up again and another hole is dug. The flat boat returns and its passengers spill out and wander along to watch too. I can make the next boat if I go now, but I'm reluctant to leave.

All eyes are on the fifteen clothes lines springing up – except for me. Needing a toilet, I scan the grounds.

The singlet man is still talking to Miss Dark Hair. Looking past them, I spy a toilet block nearby. He suddenly pushes her hard into the tree. I blink, trying to process what I've seen, my heart thumping hard. Someone's head blocks my view of her.

The siren gets louder.

The blonde teacher is laughing at something Mr White Shirt says.

Am I the only one who sees?

I push my way through the growing crowd searching for Miss Dark Hair. By the time I get clear, she's slumped to the ground against the gumtree. Dark red stains the front of her white blouse. Notebooks are scattered around her. The singlet man runs and disappears behind the umbrellas.

Miss Blondie screams.

***

2

Escape

I can't take it anymore.

Terry tries to snuggle against me but I push him off. "For god's sake, you stink." My outburst turns into regret and hangs there in the stillness. The sadness in his dark round eyes pierces me with guilt before he slinks off and slumps into the opposite corner. Everywhere he goes he leaves a foul scent. I can't bear him. But at least I know he'll bury himself in remorse and keep away for an hour or two.

My stomach rumbles. The day is fading fast. For some reason I'm mesmerised by the dust picking its way through the dying light. I lift my head and strain to listen. Somewhere behind the wall is the comforting hum of machinery. The bustle of footsteps outside seems to have quietened. Surely it's time for dinner.

Minnie wanders across and moans. "Can't you do something? I'm so, so sad."

It's typical of her. She hasn't been here long, yet she whinges and cries the most. The others ignore her.

I haul myself up and stare into her milky green eyes. "What do you expect me to do? Just shut up," I snap.

"There's no need to be so mean." She sniffs then skulks across to Terry.

In the beginning I didn't understand. I thought it was temporary, that I'd be free. I've been here so long; I can barely remember not being here. When I think hard, I can visualise my mother's desperate grey eyes. Too many mouths to feed. Scrawny herself. What choice did she have?

I walk with purpose to the other end then walk back again as if on patrol. Minnie is silent, head bowed.

Suddenly, I'm hit in the back with a thud so hard

I sprawl to the floor. The wind is knocked out of me. Beth's playful grin pops up. She's so close to my face I smell her hot putrid breath. Her eyelashes move fast.

"Get off me, you idiot."

"C'mon. Don't be a spoilsport," she says, before jumping off me. "There's nothing else to do."

Beth is the happy optimistic one. Everyone likes her. She hasn't been here long. But she's pretty and I know she'll get out before me.

Pulling myself up, Bobby pushes me from behind. I'm spread-eagled under him. Beth jumps on him and they both roll off me and laugh.

"She's a sour one today," Bobby says. "Woke up on the wrong side of bed did we?"

"What's gotten into you?" Beth asks.

I glare at them both. "I'm sick to death of all of you. I don't want to be your friend. I don't want to talk and I don't want to muck around. Just leave me alone!"

"Hmph! Come on," Beth says, running after Bobby.

Maybe I'm jealous. I hate the way they team up together. Bobby adores Beth – you can tell. They share everything. They think a bit of playfulness is going to wipe away the pain of abandonment. They're wrong.

I have to get away, get my own place where I can do whatever I want, go wherever I please, be loved and cared for. My plan starts to take shape but my thoughts are interrupted by footsteps. We freeze and stare at the door, waiting. The ugly sour smell hits me before I see it. Food.

*

The next day, a bird props itself on the window ledge and looks down at us. The sky is blue and I'm beginning to feel hot in the morning sun. Breakfast is small but I don't feel much like eating. I'm nervous. I know they'll come today. I'm resolved in my plan. The smell of Terry passing by makes me retch. I give Beth and Bobby a warning look and ignore Minnie's incessant cries.

I check myself. Long hair washed and groomed? Check. Nails clean? Check. Ears and face clean? Check. Now for my smile – I practice and practice while I wait.

"What are you doing to your face?" Beth giggles.

"Nothing. Mind your own business." Beth nudges Bobby and they snigger.

Finally, the door opens and I see them. Two. I

scan their smiling faces. I've decided. They're the ones. Now to convince them. With my big, round eyes, I stare at them, willing them to look at me. We make eye contact. A smile of excitement from the smallest one, who speaks to the bigger one. They nod. If only I can understand what they're saying. I use my big eyes to signal them. As they circle me, I try to follow. If only I can reach out, but the glass wall separates us.

Minnie cries out, "I'm here! Take me."

I turn around and hiss, "Shut up. You're ruining everything."

She wails.

Beth and Bobby begin their acrobatic show. The two are watching and pointing.

I panic.

Beth and Bobby are tumbling. I wait and jump on top of them using them as my base. I lift my head and catch the eye of the smallest one before losing my balance and unceremoniously plummeting to the ground. Beth and Bobby jump on top of me. With all my strength, I fight out of the scrum then look around.

Where are they? My plan is disintegrating. I turn around and around in circles. They've gone.

I sigh and look across at Beth and Bobby. They're worn out and almost asleep. I'm exhausted too and lay down to rest.

As I drift off, hands grip me. I open an eye and the face of the smallest one stares down at me, smiling. She pulls me close and I inhale her sweet smell. I'm surrounded by her warmth and, at last, feel safe and free.

Then I do what any self-respecting feline would do, and promptly fall asleep.

***

3

When I Really, Truly Have To.

It's cold and windy. Another typical winter's day. I've been putting it off for too long and have done everything but the thing that's the hardest. Now there's no excuse. The performance is three days away. I have to sew her outfit and what I need is on top of the cupboard. That's where I store all sorts of things I don't want cluttering the place but haven't the heart to throw away. After all, you never know when you might need a certain something. That dress I'd saved had come in handy for the eighties party last year.

The problem is the stuff on the top of the cupboard is hard to get at. I only venture there when I really truly have to. But there's no getting away from it. Settling the sewing kit on the bed, I open the cupboard door.

Climbing onto a chair I've pulled across, I feel along the dusty surface. Standing on tip toes, I spy a roll of sequinned fabric lying in the corner and curse my mother for my lack of height.

Reaching up, muscles stretched tight, I walk my fingers and pull an edge of the fabric inch by inch until I can grip the end of the roll and hold it in my hand. Throwing it onto the bed it lands on the edge and unravels in a stream of colour across the floor.

Before getting down, I glance across the shelf and see the wooden box just within reach. Forgetting about what I should be doing, I nudge the box into my arms.

Ignoring the stream of fabric making a path across the floor, I sit in an armchair nearby, cradling the box as if it were a newborn baby. My fingers flutter across the wooden carving of a house, lion and butterfly etched into the lid. Flowers adorn the corners. What had the artist intended? A Chinese arched bridge with smaller butterflies is carved along the side. The brass clasp with its keyhole holds the lid in place but the lock has long gone.

What am I doing? The fabric taunts me. I have a garment to make. There's no time for this. But the butterfly urges me to open the lid.

A bundle of cards lies on top. I finger the satin pink ribbon tied tenderly around the well wishes and sympathies given not so many years ago. The eulogy I'd written lay there – a limp reminder of my orphaned state.

I should have placed it all back and snapped the lid shut. Instead, blinking back tears, I place the bundle on the upturned lid.

Next is a plastic bag. Grinning, I reach in and pull out a pony tail of thick black hair still held together by its pink hair tie. When I was ten, my thick, knotted hair hung down to my waist. The hairdresser had carefully combed it before cutting it all off, leaving my head feeling like a balloon connected by a string. My mother had saved my locks and presented them to me on my eighteenth birthday. I return the remnant of my childhood to the bag and place it tenderly next to the bundle.

Next is a cream-coloured envelope with my

name handwritten in ink by someone I can't remember. Peeking inside, I pull out a photo. The waterfall in the background brings back the heat and smell of the rainforest. My hair was short and wavy then, legs in denim shorts, long and lean. In the photo, I'm standing next to a man whose thongs are poking out from beneath the hem of his dark flared pants. His bare arm, wrapped around my waist, masks his finger's harsh prod. My unsmiling face bears a pain I thought was hidden. I tear the photo into tiny pieces to be discarded forever.

The last thing in the box is a package wrapped in brown paper tied with raffia. I untie the bow –– pink and blue, faded and worn. Closing my eyes, I whisper, "Tinka, my friend." Without thinking, I nestle her against my cheek, remembering her smell and my protests when my mother had wrenched her from me to wash. Clean once again, I rubbed her along my body and in my hair to bring back her smell. Hurt and disappointment disappeared; joy and calm enticed itself out of me. I sniff. Her smell isn't as I remember. Stale and foreign.

"Mummy ... Mummy... Mummy ..." sings the

voice from somewhere on the other side of my house.

I stiffen and ready my smile, listening to my small daughter's footsteps clatter along the wooden floor. Banging the door wide open, she bursts in and dances across the floor in her fairy dress.

"Mummy! Wook, wook." She twirls around and around.

"What a clever girl you are. Have you shown Daddy?"

"No! You see."

"OK, Louisa. One more time and then you should show Daddy too. We don't want him to miss out do we?"

She twirls again grabbing the sequinned fabric and trails it in arms held high above her head. Then she sees what's clutched in my hands. Dropping the fabric, she snatches Tinka from me with blustering curiosity.

"Be very careful," I say, too late.

A small pink and blue arm has been wrenched from Tinka's body. Oblivious, Louisa speaks in a language known only to her. But, like I had once done, she rubs the small bear against her face and takes in its comfort.

As suddenly as she's arrived, Louisa is gone with a twirl of her dress, Tinka, thrown to the floor.

I repack the box and place Tinka gently on the armchair. Her damaged arm lies still in my hand. I find my needle and thread and roll up the fabric. Soon, Tinka is mended. With a quick kiss I wrap and tuck her into the box, sliding it back into the far corner of the cupboard.

Pushing the chair back, I glance out of the window then at my watch.

The rain has stopped; droplets shine like diamonds on the tree outside. The sky is blue. Maybe a quick walk with Louisa before I start?

***

4

Nosy

It was late and I'd almost forgotten. The garbage bin rolled with ease to rest on the footpath. I glanced up and down the quiet street. All of the houses were dark except for Martha's. I'd never seen a rubbish bin on her overgrown footpath. Even in the dim street light, I could tell that her front gate was hanging on one hinge and the shadows rolling down the walls were peeling paint. Her house was an eyesore.

"You'd think she'd fix her place up. It's a disgrace," Dot whined when she cornered me one day at the mail box. "I'm going to lodge a complaint."

"Maybe she can't afford to fix it," I said.

"Rubbish," Dot said as she turned to go back to her pristine, painted, white picket gate. "She's loaded."

I quickly brushed the cobwebs off my own white letterbox.

How she knew the state of Martha's finances was anybody's guess. But now, in the dark, I wondered what was behind the lit window opposite.

Scanning the street again and I tiptoed across the road, through the front gate, and crouched under the filthy window with its torn lace curtains.

I heard footsteps approaching: clip clop, clip clop, and a ball bouncing on the footpath. I smiled to myself. Basketball Boy was out late again. That was what I called him. I didn't actually know him or where he lived. But he'd bounce his basketball as he walked down the street, late, every night.

What was I thinking? I should have been in bed reading my book right now. Instead, I was caught behind a bush, which had never been touched by a set of pruning shears, waiting for Basketball Boy to pass so I could look into the old lady's house. I rubbed my bare arms in the chill. I could have knocked on the door and introduced myself in the light of day, but there was no going back.

The noise of the basketball got louder as it neared. It wasn't a cold night yet my teeth chattered. Crouching lower in the dirt, I hugged my knees close and gently rocked to the beat. Bounce, bounce, bounce.

Something moved inside the house. The window above me opened and I froze. A whiff of warm, rotting faeces drifted into my nostrils, and my stomach churned. My heart beat faster than the thud of the bouncing ball, now only two or three houses away. Bang. Bang. Bang.

Looking up, I met two glistening, silvery eyes, their gaze crawling over me like bugs. Involuntarily, I squeaked. The bouncing stopped. Surely the whole neighbourhood could hear the pounding in my chest? I held my breath.

"C'mon, c'mon," Basketball Boy whispered coaxingly. Was he talking to me? My legs ached but I daren't move from behind the shrub despite the twig sticking hard into my back. My mind went blank as I tried to think of what to say if I was caught.

"C'mon," he whispered again. He wandered up

the old lady's path, the ball under his arm, and held out his hand. He was so close; I could smell his sweat.

The eyes glistened above me, the cat silhouetted against the light from inside. Would it give me away? The boy stepped closer. Toward the window and my hiding spot. Time dragged.

"Get out of 'ere," a croaky voice yelled.

I cowered, unable to move. Who was she talking to? The boy ran off. The cat ducked back inside and the window slammed shut, taking the stench with it.

Finally, I let out the breath I'd been holding and unwound from my crouch. Sneaking across the road, I crept into my own house, into my own warm bed, and welcomed the hint of lavender from my freshly laundered sheets.

"Where have you been?" my sleeping man murmured.

"Just putting the bins out," I whispered.

★★★

5

Revenge

I'm aghast when I wake up and stare into the mirror. More pimples on my chin. It's too soon to squeeze them, so I rummage through my armoury of makeup and pad on the foundation until all I can see is a lumpy silhouette.

"Get out!" my older sister, Charlotte, screams. "I've gotta pee."

With a savage push, she barrels me out of the bathroom. 'Shitface,' I mutter. Even though I expect it, I still flinch when she slams the door and locks it. At that moment I hate her more than anything. I stare at the door knowing she's using my make-up.

As usual, I try to plot revenge while I get ready for school. But my burgeoning pimples worry me more.

"C'mon idiot," Charlotte screeches. "Dad's waiting."

"Shut up. I'm coming," I say under my breath. I hate the way she speaks to me.

I shove stuff in my school bag then pick up my homework sheet: due on Wednesday 23rd. That's today! I gulp back panic as my stepmother barges in.

"What are you doing? Can't you hear the car horn?" I shove the homework sheet in and drag my bag along the floor.

"I'm coming," I say strolling into the kitchen to grab a glass of water.

"Get going!" My stepmother stands watching me with her hands on her hips, like a guard, except she's still in her nightie. I stop myself from telling her what I think.

"Have you got your learners?" she screams from the front door as I haul my bag into the car.

"Yes!" Charlotte yells from the driver's seat.

"Seatbelt on pumpkin?" Dad twists himself

around and smiles at me while Charlotte starts the car.

"Dad! We're going to be late again. All because of her."

"OK. Now concentrate on driving."

I pull out my phone and lose myself in Facebook.

When we arrive, Charlotte elbows me out of the way to get to her friends. I hate them too. They have their own common room and prance around the school thinking they're above everyone, bellyaching how VCE is so hard.

School's hard. Haven't they worked that out yet?

I'm glad to see my best friend, Emma. "Late again?" she says. "The bell's just rung."

"Yeah, Charlotte was being a bitch. Made me late."

"What's she done this time?"

"See that?" I pull my sleeve up and show her the bruise on my arm.

"Slut."

"I've got to think of a way to get back at her. I'm sick of it." But I'm soon distracted by having to run to class.

At lunch with Emma I eat my vegemite sandwich and we begin to plot.

"Look at her and her friends," I say. "They think they're so good. Maybe I can set fire to her."

"Nah, she'd stink too much. Ugh, burning flesh. What about telling your dad she's preggers? She'd get kicked out of home for sure then." We giggle.

"Yeah, good idea."

"Hey girls. Wattya got there. How about a chip?"

I look up and the sun is blocked by someone standing behind me.

"Piss off, Hayden. Get your own," Emma says grabbing the chip bag she's just opened.

Hayden sits next to me and I hover my hand over my chin. The boys from St. Anthony's Boys Grammar next door sometimes use our school facilities. I'm pleased to see him.

"Shouldn't you be going?" Emma says.

"You wanna go to the formal?"

I reach into the chip bag. I knew his school was having a formal and was secretly pleased he'd asked me.

"Well?" he says.

"Yeah, OK. Might be fun I suppose."

He manages to steal a chip just as he gets up. "OK then. See you later," he says. He turns and makes a face, "Oh and thanks for the chip Em."

"What did you say yes for? He's such a loser."

"I may as well go."

"You're gonna have to buy another dress," Emma says.

I hadn't thought about that. I can't wear last year's one.

"Maybe I'll wear one of Charlotte's dresses. She's got plenty."

"Well, you'll have to put up with her then."

The bell rings.

"Shit," I say, trudging back to class worrying about what to wear.

*

A couple of weeks later, Hayden asks me to meet him at our local shopping centre. He wants help picking out a tie to match my dress for the formal. I still don't have anything to wear and time's running out but I don't tell him that.

Before I meet Hayden, I rummage through Charlotte's wardrobe and try on a few of her dresses while she pretends to do what she calls work at McDonalds. They're all pretty ugly but I settle on a purple one that I know doesn't fit her anymore.

"Come on. Let's go," Dad yells from the front

door. "If you want a ride you better come now ... I've got to pick up Charlotte."

I rush around getting ready, grab the dress and shove it in a bag to take with me.

"Dad, can you me drop at Chaddy first? I'm already late," I say.

"No, love. McDonalds is on the way. It'll only be a few minutes."

"Please, dad. I'm going to be sooo late."

But Dad ignores me and as he drives into the carpark, Charlotte is pacing out the front. She looks mad. To my amazement, Dad gets out of the car and my sister slides into the driver's seat.

"Come on, love," Dad says opening the front passenger door expecting me to move.

"But Dad. I'm going to be even later," I grumble getting out and into the back.

"We won't be long."

"Why can't she drive after you've dropped me off?"

"Shut up," Charlotte says flinging her L plate toward me expecting me to stick it to the rear window.

Texts roll on my phone. "WTF", "Where R U?" It's Hayden. "COMING NOW" I reply.

"Is that my dress?" Charlotte says. In my hurry, I haven't stuffed her dress properly in the bag on the back seat. She starts the car.

"Oh yeah. I'm borrowing it. For the formal."

"No, you're not." My sister looks into the rear view mirror.

She gives way then accelerates.

"Watch your speed. Now, put your blinker on to turn right."

"If you had of asked I would have let you borrow it. But since you've stolen it, you can't have it."

"You can't wear it anymore. It doesn't even fit you. I can't afford to buy another one," I whine.

"You're too far into the intersection. Now stop talking and concentrate. Go after that blue car."

"I know how to drive, Dad."

"I'm taking it." I have the plastic bag in my hand ready to jump out of the car. I text Hayden that I'll meet him in five minutes at Hungry Jacks.

"No, you're not."

"Pull in over there. Blinker on," Dad instructs.

We pull up and I open the car door. As I'm getting out, something pulls me back. It's Charlotte's hand on the bag.

"Give it back," she hisses.

"Dad, tell her to let go of me."

Dad turns and she lets go. "Charlotte! Concentrate! Look at the sign. It's no standing. We have to go." He's looking at the sign but she's giving me a look of death.

I barely have time to get out before Charlotte takes off. And then I fall onto the pavement screaming in pain. My foot has somehow got caught under the tyre.

Dad must have seen me because the car stops. He jumps out of the car and kneels next to me. I'm still screaming and can see my sister's horrified face above me. She's crying now and watches anxiously over me. "I'm sorry. I'm sorry. It was an accident," she says.

I try to compose myself when I see other faces I don't know. I want them to go. Somebody offers to call an ambulance. A large woman in a flowery dress is trying to check my foot but I pull it away. They talk about me as if I'm not there.

"Is she OK?"

"Is it broken?"

"How did it happen?"

"Is she alright? I heard her scream."

Dad helps me get up. All I can do is stand on one

foot and lean against him. I wipe my nose on my sleeve and a tissue is shoved into my hand. "Here you go, love. Poor thing."

Dad is holding me up. Then to the crowd of gawkers, he says, "It's alright. She'll be fine. We better go and get her to the hospital."

"It really, really hurts," I whimper, wondering if I'll ever walk again.

Charlotte grabs my other arm and whispers into my ear. "I'm really sorry. You can have the dress if you like."

With Dad and Charlotte on either side of me, I hobble into the back seat. Charlotte sits beside me and cradles my foot in her lap. We're both sobbing and Dad takes control of the wheel.

*

At the hospital, the doctor looks happy with himself. "You're very lucky you were wearing those Blundstone boots. Nothing broken just a bit of bruising to the heel."

"Do I need crutches?"

"Just for a couple of days. It's a good idea to keep off your feet."

I'm mulling over how this whole thing is going to affect me when the bombshell hits.

"But I've got a formal in a week. Can I still wear high heels?" I don't remember what he says because then I remember Hayden. "Shit! What time is it? Where's my phone? Quick."

"It's probably still in the car," Dad says. "It wasn't on the footpath. Was it?"

"Oh no!" I start crying again.

"I'll go and get it," Charlotte says gently squeezing my arm.

"Here you are. Try these for size," the doctor orders. "Are you still in pain? The painkillers should work very soon," he says, mistaking the reason for my tears.

As I hobble out of the hospital entrance on my crutches, Charlotte is running up from the carpark with my phone in her hand.

"Stay with her while I get the car," Dad says, sitting me on a bench just outside the hospital's front door.

There are about twenty missed calls and texts. I ring Hayden. Charlotte wanders off while I explain.

"Look, I'm really sorry but my sister ran over my foot."

"Yeah?" he says.

"It's the truth. But I'm alright. The doctor said

that I only need to be on crutches for a couple of days."

"I waited for more than an hour."

"I'm really sorry. I can go with you tomorrow, if you like."

"I know you didn't really want to go."

"But I do want to go. Really I do."

"Don't worry about it. I've asked someone else," he says.

"Oh. OK," is all I can say, and we hang up. I didn't really like him too much anyway.

Charlotte comes back and holds out an extra-large Cherry Ripe; her eyes beg for my forgiveness. "I'm really, really sorry. I got you this." I unwrap it and sink my teeth into it – my favourite.

"It's alright. It was an accident." I can say it now that the pain killers have kicked in. "I don't need to borrow your dress anymore." I tell her what Hayden said.

"That bastard. I'll punch his lights out Monday."

When we get home, my sister can't do enough for me. Even my stepmother sprays me with affection. I'm beginning to enjoy the attention. I ring Emma and tell her what happened.

"You've got your revenge now," she says.

"What do you mean?" I say.

"Her guilt for running over you is going to last a really long time."

"Yeah ... Yeah it is." I nod and smile.

***

6

The Nut

The seaside town of Stanley in Northern Tasmania with its quaint workers' cottages preserved from a century-old era, is pretty. The streetscape is dominated by The Nut, a giant flat rock plonked right behind it. The only way to walk up its steep slope is on my toes. At the top, a gentle breeze cools off my sweat and I admire the view of the town on one side and the ocean on the other.

"Now, I know why they call it the edge of the world. It sure feels like it," I say.

"Did you know, The Nut used to be the core of a volcano?" my husband, Brian reads out from the guide. "The Van Dieman's Land Company was granted this land in 1825."

"I wonder what happened to the Aborigines who lived here?" I ask.

"Dunno. It doesn't say," he shrugs. "Do you want to go for a wander? We have to stick to the paths. They reckon people have got lost up here and never been seen again."

"I can't think of a nicer place to get lost in," I say, trying to post a photo on Facebook. "Damn! There's no reception."

In the afternoon, we take a cruise boat to watch the seals who seem bored as the diesel smoke swirls around them. The Nut stands protectively over the town.

"Imagine what it must be like in winter," Brian says pulling his coat around him.

After a full day of touring, we go back and sit on the veranda of our rented cottage to enjoy a cool drink while admiring the aurora over the bay.

"Don't you think the candles are a nice touch?" I'd found several tea lights and scattered them inside and outside.

"Yeah I s'pose," Brian says glancing up from the

iPad. "They reckon it only ever happens here once or twice a year."

"Stop squinting at the iPad. Why don't you look at the flashes of red, orange and purple out there?" He's an academic even on a holiday. "Let's go for a walk along the beach."

But his head is back in whatever he's reading. I give up and finish my drink.

"I think I'll stroll down to the beach," I say "Do you want to come or not?"

"You go," he says. "I think I'll stay here."

I know he has a blister from his ill-fitting shoes. But it's his fault he refused to go back and change them before our earlier walk.

"Ok," I say. "I won't be too long. I want to get a better shot from the beach."

He grunts and nods in the glow of the screen.

Crossing the road, I find the footpath and meander along the beach's edge. I pull the iPhone from the pocket of my jeans, snap the changing sky then upload it onto Instagram to make my friends jealous. The Nut looms like a giant shadow behind our cottage and there is Brian, head bowed, surrounded by twinkling tea lights.

No-one seems to be around except for the

seagulls dotted along the shoreline. A four-foot marker is plonked in the middle of the path, demanding attention. I stop to read the inscription.

In 1842, 90 km south-west of here, the last recorded capture of a Tasmanian aboriginal family took place. The family was delivered to the Van Diemen's Land Company for a bounty.

Imagining their anguished screams of desperation saddens me.

Suddenly, I find myself in a whirlwind of leaves and debris and fight my way out to a park bench nearby. I sit and admire the sky's dying light.

A dark-skinned woman in a long flowery dress walks by then doubles back to sit at the end of the bench.

"Nice evening?" she says.

"Yes. Yes, it is," I say rubbing the tightness from my aching calves.

I sense her fidgeting but I'm too polite to stare in her direction.

"You better get out of here," she says softly. "It's not a good place."

For some reason I can't make out her face – the sunset behind her casts her in shadow.

"What? Why?"

She gets up suddenly. "Quick," she whispers looking around her. "We better go."

Before I realise what's happening, she grabs my arm and pulls me up. I'm surprised by her strong grip.

"What's going on?"

"Quick. Run."

Panicked, I run, even though I have no idea what or who I'm running from. Soon my chest hurts and I'm puffing hard. Somehow I'm back on the same path up to The Nut.

"I have to ... I have to stop," I say, twisting my hand from her grip. I try to look behind me, but she grabs me again and starts running. Older than me, I wonder how she has the energy. She seems to fly on her feet.

"Wait!" I puff. "What are we running from?"

She slows. "There's no time. Come."

When we're close to the top, she lets me stop to get my breath.

"Listen. I don't know who you are or what you're on about," I gasp. "I don't know why I'm even with you. But I've already climbed this godforsaken bloody rock once today and if you don't mind, I'm going back. It's dark and my husband's probably wondering where I am."

"Too dangerous." She isn't even puffed. When I try again to twist away from her, she grips me even tighter. The path is so steep that she stands above me. I feel small and helpless.

"Who the hell are you?"

"I'm Martha. We must go," she whispers. Her face is so close to mine I smell stale onions on her breath. "It's not safe."

She jogs me up the path until I think my chest is going to burst. But there's no rest when we reach the top. We pass the lookout, where I'd stood earlier, and veer off the path into the bush. I wonder who the people are who were lost and never found again and wonder if my name will be added to the list. But Martha seems to know where she's going as she winds her way through the scrub. Then, we stop. The fizz of stale gin and tonic bursts from my mouth, burning my nose. I can't stop heaving.

"Please," I say finally, barely able to speak. "I have to get back."

"We must keep going."

Stumbling in the dark, we climb down a rocky

path. Branches slice into my bare arms. I think I hear the echo of sirens.

Finally, she pushes aside a bush and pulls me into a cave. Leading me into the darkness, she sits me down gently on something soft. Then releases my hand.

*

I cough awake. Lying on a lumpy mattress, I watch smoke spiralling from the flames of crackling twigs. Welcoming the warmth on my face, I listen. Somewhere outside waves crash desperately. I rub my burning eyes. Something is thrust between my dry lips. Pausing for breath, I notice the smile playing on the lips of the woman who I remember is Martha. The flames from the fire glisten on her white teeth.

I hear my own quivering voice. "Uh, where am I?" I sit up, tip my head back and stare at the shadows on the rocky ceiling. A black spider scurries into a crevice. "I have to get going. Thanks for the drink." Why am I being so polite?

Martha squats and throws a large piece of wood on the fire. "There is nowhere else for you to go. You are safest here with us."

I blink and look around the cave. Another woman and a young boy lie asleep.

"Thanks. But I have to go. My husband will be worried." I try to stand up but I scrape my head against a low rocky outcrop.

"It's too dark. It's not safe."

"I'll be fine," I say, feeling around in my pocket for my mobile phone. "There's a torch in this. See."

Her bulbous dark eyes stare back at me.

"Well, it looks like it's flat. Um ... what time is it?"

"Maybe dawn soon. Sit down. I'll make tea."

A billy on the fire soon gurgles and Martha hands me a mug of black tea. I want a drop of milk but say nothing as I sip. I can't believe this is happening.

"What am I doing here?" I ask. "I'm grateful you felt I needed saving but I'm not in danger. I'm just a tourist."

Martha shakes her head and mumbles. I study her weathered face in the firelight. It's kind and full of understanding. Her thinning hair, streaked with grey and frizz falls like a wispy curtain around her shoulders. Somehow my instincts tell me I can trust her.

"Pardon?" I say.

She stares at me. "You are safe here. I will tell

you when you can go. Try and rest." Is it sympathy that crosses her face? For some reason, I'm not scared.

She lays down on the floor in the dirt of the cave and I drain my mug.

Now what? She's right. I can't get back on my own. I have no idea where I am. My burning eyes droop and exhaustion sweeps over me.

*

Something taps my shoulder. I open my eyes. A small boy stares at me. Blonde curly hair falls over his olive face and his grin shows off the gap where his front teeth should be.

"She's awake!" he declares, running off.

The fire has died but sunshine filters through the gap of the cave's mouth.

Every part of my body aches and I rub my neck. My hands are clammy and I stink of stale smoke. Pushing my way through the bush hiding the cave's entrance, I breathe in the cool freshness of the day. The sun has risen over the sea and the boy sits in the clearing next to a woman who, I presume, is his mother. She stops rolling up a blanket as she sees me and glances at Martha who turns and smiles.

"It's safe now. I'll take you back." She moves

towards me and takes my hands gently in hers. The red nail polish I'd applied only yesterday is already badly chipped. She turns my dirt-caked hands over, stares at my palms then looks deep into my eyes. "You're going to be alright." Releasing my hands, she turns, expecting me to follow.

"I'm very confused," I say, chasing after her. But she walks so fast I give up trying to get any sense from her.

Soon we reach a path. Martha turns abruptly and points. "You go that way."

I stare at the path then turn to thank her but she's already gone.

My legs are wobbling like jelly by the time I reach the town. There's no-one around on the streets, which I think is odd since the sun is high in the sky. Glancing into one of the shop windows, I'm shocked by my reflection. I try to push the wildness of my hair into place. I look a sight with scratch marks down my arms and blackened hands and feet. What happened to my shoes? My stomach rumbles and my teeth feel furry. I badly want a hot shower. How can I to explain my absence when I can't understand what's happened?

Brian must be at the police station but I don't

know where it is. I decide to go back to our rented cottage.

Only when I turn the bend I stop, stunned. The building is a shell of its former self. I find my feet and run. Where is Brian? Two men stand near the burnt out carcass that was our car. I recognise the blackened iPad cover held by one man – it's Brian's.

"What's happened?" I pant. "Where's my husband?"

They swing around. A tall narrow man squints. "Are you Josie Green?"

I nod. The older, thickset man reaches for my arm. "Listen, love. We've been looking all over for you. We thought you must have ... you know, got caught in the fire." He jerks his head toward the house. I roll his sentence around in my head, confused.

"I don't know what you're talking about," I say. "Do you know where my husband is?"

"Come along, love." The men take up position on either side of me and lead me gently away from the house. "We better take you to the hospital to get you checked out." I catch the pitying look they exchange, and I don't like it.

"Listen, what's going on here? I'm not going anywhere until you tell me where my husband is." Panic is rising and my chest pounds. "Everyone in this town is stark raving mad. I'm tired and hungry and now I'm angry." My voice is beginning to rise. "So you better give me some answers – right now!" Then I hear a woman's screams, deep in my head. Mine. I'm out of control.

"There, there love."

"Don't you patronise me!" I yell.

"You've had a fright. We're going to take care of you."

"For the last time I do not need to be taken care of. Now, are you going to tell me where Brian is? Better still, take me to the police station. Does the landlord know his house has burnt down? He's probably there organising a report for the insurance company. Heaven knows how we'll get back. I don't suppose you know if there is another car rental company here?" I can't bear the look of pity.

"Where have you been?" the taller man quietly asks.

"You're supposed to be answering my questions not asking them," I yell. I shake off their hands and walked briskly in the direction of the beach. The men follow.

"Josie. Josie. We're here to help."

"This place is unbelievable. Who are you anyway?" I yell.

"I'm Constable Wright and this is Constable Harvey. Don't you remember we told you before? Josie do you think you can stop? Just for a minute?"

I stop, overwhelmed.

"Oh," I say. "Look, I'm really sorry." I'm crying now, telling them about Martha. "So you see," I sniff, "I'm a bit overwrought over the kidnapping and now I come back to all of this." I can't help notice a knowing glance between the men.

"What?" I dab my eyes with a man-sized hanky wondering how I got it.

"Josie, let's just sit down here. About that woman Martha, she lived here many years ago. But she doesn't live here anymore." He's talking to me as if I'm slow witted. Like there's something wrong with me.

"You don't understand. It must be some other Martha." I begin crying again. Why isn't anyone listening to me?

I let them lead me to a seat. A brass plaque is screwed into the back. The inscription reads "In memory of Martha Clements 1842." I glance along the path and see the headstone. It's the same seat I'd sat on yesterday.

***

7

The Black Satin Pants

I'm reluctant to extricate myself from the stale warmth of the tram, but I force my way out into the pelting rain. My umbrella does little to shelter me and my feet somehow find a puddle in the gutter. I run on my toes but the bottom of my skirt is soaked by the time I reach the red and gold painted doorway. There, I shake off the rain, deposit my pathetic excuse for an umbrella and walk in as if I own the place.

I'm struck by the warmth and the smell of freshly brewed coffee, which I search for amongst the racks of old clothes and bric-a-brac. I stop to feel the soft red velvet of a dress. The tag says House of Merivale. Definitely late seventies, I think.

"May I help you?"

Smelling musky perfume, I swing around and face a middle-aged woman with dyed black hair. Her face, lined with powder-caked crevices, tremors when she speaks. "May I help you?" I decide she's a refugee from the past and doesn't realise it's 2016.

"Ah, yes my name is Anita and I'm here about the pants. I rang earlier?"

She squints her blue-smeared plump eyelids as if I'm speaking another language.

"The black satin pants?" I say. "I spoke to Meryl or Mary or some name like that."

She breaks out into a wide smile of recognition and I glimpse the silver tongue stud curtained by her yellow teeth.

"Oh yes. The black pants. That was me. I'm Marina. I spoke to you yesterday."

She turns, expecting me to follow. Leaving sodden footsteps, I pick my way through the maze of racks and shelves to the overcrowded counter. The dust permeates my nostrils and I stifle a sneeze.

"Here it is," she says excitedly.

Marina brings out a package wrapped in tissue paper. Two other women, dressed in black leather skirts and colourful tops, appear to watch the grand unveiling. I hold my breath, hardly able to contain my own excitement.

"They're magnificent," says one woman.

"They are, aren't they," Marina says, gently holding out the black bundle to me.

"Yes. Yes," I say, letting the garment unravel to reveal the gold buttons on the side pockets. The length of the heavy satin fabric falls to a wide flare. A gold lame belt is looped through the waistband. The label inside seems authentic and the size looks right. I can hardly believe my luck.

"Would you like to try them on?" Marina whispers. I nod and she shows me to the changing room with its dirty, flimsy curtain. Flinging off my damp skirt and shoes, I'm careful to keep them well away from my prize. Holding the pants up from the dusty concrete floor, I squeeze myself into them one leg after the other.

"How are you going?" Marina asks from the other side.

"Yep. All good."

The zip glides easily and I clip the gold clasp at my waist then pull the belt into the last notch.

Now for the mirror. There is none. I'm forced to leave the sanctity of the change room and step into a semi-circle of shop assistants. I'm annoyed they see the fit before I can. I tiptoe about hoping the flares aren't touching the floor. Marina steers me to the mirror.

"They fit you like a glove. Like they were made for you." She looks at the assistants, who murmur and nod their heads in approval. I wish I could savour the moment alone.

"What about a nice crop top?"

"Thanks. I've got one," I say.

Suddenly a pair of red and gold glittered platforms is thrust at me. "Here, you have to have these. Try them on."

I raise my eyebrows when I spy the label and slip them on.

"They're circa mid to late eighties," she says apologetically, "But I think they work. Don't you?"

The other two nod.

"Thanks," I say.

"You could take these down a smidge," Marina says checking the length of the pants.

The flares cover most of the shoes, which I glimpse as I turn to admire my pear-shaped rear. My hands glide over the fabric. "Yes," I say to no-one in particular, taking one last look before heading back into the hovel of a dressing room.

When I hang the pants carefully on a hanger, something resembling a ticket stub falls out of the pocket. I push it into my purse before dressing in my damp clothes.

Marina is chatting to a customer when I wander up to the counter holding the pants and the shoes. I hand over my credit card, deciding that I'll worry later how I'm going to pay off the equivalent of a week's salary.

The cloud has lifted along with my mood by the time I reach my apartment. Flinging off my clothes, I rummage through my bottom draw. I bring out the top and hold it to my face. I swear I can still smell a faint perfume. Undoing my bra, I throw it on the bed then carefully pull the red and black sequined top over my head. I tie the halter ends around my neck and unroll the bodice until it almost reaches my belly button. I push my breasts into place. My heart pounds with excitement as I pull on the pants, put on the shoes, then stare at myself in the mirror. I blink back the tears.

Removing the pants, I examine them in minute detail. A plastic zip replaces what once would have been the original metal one. A small part of the hem is down to its former length. Pulling gently, I undo some of the stitching. The hem, redone by hand in a herringbone stitch, had been taken up by a couple of centimetres. I retry the pants for the extra length, then check the pockets. A one cent piece is wedged at the bottom of one but, disappointingly, nothing else. Then I remember the stub which I remove from my purse. The words are faded: Festival Hall: David Essex. I squint at the date: 1976.

*

Kim found a desk at the back of the hot, stuffy portable classroom and smiled weakly at her best friend, Jenny, who rolled her eyes and mouthed, "Take a look at him."

Mr Henderson pulled up his brown pants as high as he could, his bony round shoulders protruding through his discoloured white shirt. He coughed for everyone's attention. Kim stifled a giggle as she opened her notebook.

His droning voice soon faded amongst the chirping of birds outside and Kim slumped over the desk, doodling circles on her notebook.

She wasn't in the mood to concentrate. How was she going to convince her parents to let her go to the concert? She loved David Essex. What girl didn't? Everyone was going and she wasn't about to miss out. Jenny had got the tickets and given them to her at recess: Friday 20 April 1976. Kim's dad wasn't happy; said she wasn't doing enough. But she'd been studying for hours each day, she'd argued. She needed a break. Her father wanted her to get into Monash Engineering. "Be the first girl in the family to be an engineer, just like her old man," he'd sprout off to anyone who'd listen.

She vowed to convince her parents by getting high marks in the Maths test next week. Surely they'd let her go then. Not that it meant much. The final exam in November was the only thing that counted in HSC.

"Give me an example of the supply and demand rule. Kim?"

She jumped.

"Ah, err, ah ..."

"Sir, if there's a shortage of cigarettes and

everyone wants them then the price is going to be high," a lanky boy with long dark hair answered cheekily.

"That's right, Steve. Kim, you might do well to study that rule."

She squirmed under the teacher's penetrating stare. When Mr Henderson turned to write on the board, Kim shot Steve a look of thanks. He smiled and winked.

The bell went. Time to go home and study hard.

*

"Anita. Anita."

My younger sister, Ella bursts into my bedroom, stops and claps her hand over her mouth.

"Jesus! You look ..." Ella frowns. "Just like ... just like the photo."

"Do you think?" I say smiling.

"A dead ringer. I can't get over it." She stares at me for what seems like ages.

"Do you want me to do your make-up? You know you have to get that right. You can't go to a seventies party with modern day hair and make-up."

"Sure. If you have time. That'd be great."

She nods. "I'll get everything. Stay there."

I think back to another time. I wonder about David Essex and the holder of the ticket. And I search YouTube.

*

Kim carefully dressed – blue eyeshadow, mascara and black eyeliner. She adjusted her halter neck top and carefully applied her pink lipstick. She looked at herself critically in the mirror. Satisfied, she yelled goodbye to her mother and raced out to the waiting car. Jenny nodded approvingly.

"Are they the flares we got in Collins St? House of Merivale?" Jenny said.

"Yeah and this too." Kim adjusted her halter top and flicked back her layered blonde hair.

"I love them. You look fantastic."

"Thanks. So do you."

The girls crossed the road to join the throng of teenagers heading to Festival Hall.

They heard a wolf whistle and Jenny turned to see where it had come from.

"Not you, four eyes. Who's the spunk next to you, hey?" a pimple faced, try-hard skinhead yelled.

Kim grabbed her friend's arm sharing her embarrassment. She felt bad for Jenny. Her friend hated the black-rimmed spectacles which hid her large brown eyes.

"Get lost," Kim yelled, but her words were drowned out by the traffic.

"Bastard," Jenny muttered. "Hey, there's Steve and Rod," she said furiously waving.

They caught up to the group from school. In the crush, she lost sight of Jenny but found herself next to Steve. His arm brushed against her and she breathed in his Old Spice. His green Miller shirt and blue Levis hung nicely on his slim frame.

"C'mon. In here. Have you got your ticket?" he said. She was surprised when he grabbed her hand and pushed his way through the crowd.

"But we'll lose the others," Kim said, looking wildly around for Jenny.

"We'll find them inside," he said.

Kim reluctantly let go of his hand and fished about for the ticket in her pocket. Steve's arm brushed against her leg then settled around her waist.

"Grouse flares," he said, grinning and pulling her closer to him. Pleasure squeezed through her.

*

Anita finds the clip on YouTube and plays a song from 1976.

"Who's that?" Ella says bringing in her make-up case.

"David Essex. I found this in the pocket of the pants."

Ella examines the ticket. "Do you reckon it's been in there all this time?"

"It seems like it."

"Mm ... he's not bad," Ella says as she watches the screen. "Ugh. I don't like that song though. Now sit over here in the light so I can get the eye shadow on."

*

She was drying her eyes when Steve walked into the bedroom, which was a mess of clothes.

"You ready? Let's go," he said. "What's the matter?"

"Nothing." She picked up her bag, grabbed her jacket and he followed her out to the car.

"Well?" he said, trying to hide his impatience. "What's going on?"

"It's silly," Kim sniffed. "I tried on those black flares. You know the ones you really like."

"Yeah," he said smiling. "I love your arse in those."

"Well, I couldn't get them on. They were so tight the zip broke." She began crying again. "I'm so bloody fat now."

Steve pulled over, slid across the bench seat of the Holden Kingswood and wrapped his arms around her. "You're as beautiful as ever. I love your new curves as much as I love you." He kissed her tenderly on her eyelids and then her lips. He looked into her face as if he was looking into her very soul.

"Everything'll be great. You'll see. You're just jittery."

"Are we doing the right thing?" she said.

"Of course."

He started the car and she wondered if he was right. Not that she really wanted to be an engineer, but she said nothing. Steve winked at her as she got out of the car at Janice's unit.

"OK?" he said. She nodded to reassure him but hid her fear as he drove off to work as a night filler at Coles.

"I'm so excited," her sister squealed. "We've got lots to do. Jen's coming from Uni so she'll be a few minutes." The doorbell rang and Jen arrived with an armful of wedding magazines. "Let's get this sorted." Kim paced the lounge room.

"What's the matter?" Jenny said. "You're like a caged animal."

Kim told her sister and her best friend about the pants.

"Do either of you want them. I may as well give them away to someone who can appreciate them," Kim said.

"I don't think I'm going to get my big arse into them," Janice said. "Jen why don't you take them?"

"If you truly don't want them?" Jenny looked carefully at her friend. "I've always loved them and I'll fix them up. Are you ok if I put the hem up?"

Kim nodded and unconsciously rubbed her belly.

"Right. Now let's sort out the place settings and then the flowers," Janice said.

*

"There," Ella says surveying her handiwork. "That eyeshadow looks perfect."

I stretch my sore neck and get up to check in the full-length mirror.

"Let's do your hair ... Farah Fawcett style isn't it?"

"Yeah, lots of flicks. Look at the photo."

Ella picks up the frame on the bedside table and sighs.

"It's uncanny how much you look like her." Ella puts the photo down on the table. "Do you … do you ever wonder?"

"What?"

"Where she is? What she's doing?"

I turn back to the mirror again and sigh. "Sometimes."

"To leave us like that …" Ella is still looking at the photo. "You know I can hardly remember her. I don't know why, but I don't feel anything. Do … do you?"

I swallow the lump growing in my throat. "You were too little."

"I guess she had her reasons."

I look at Ella. "She kissed you and me, then went out to buy groceries and never came back. I'll never forget the look of hurt in Dad's face when he realised she'd planned it that way."

"Then why hunt for the pants?" Ella says. "Why dredge it up? You won't come with me to find her but you went crazy to find these pants."

"I remember Dad always talked about these pants. He fell in love with her then. I don't know.

Maybe I just wanted to touch a part of that happiness."

I don't hear what she says because suddenly, I feel as if I can't breathe.

"Don't worry about my hair. I don't feel like going now." My sister looks up sharply. I avoid her eyes. "I'm going to change."

"It's always the same with you," she calls out after me, as I head to the bathroom.

"Can you get me a make-up wipe? Quick." The waistband of the pants seems to cut into me.

"Get them yourself. They're in the second drawer," my sister calls out.

My stomach aches. My legs burn. I can't wait to get them off.

Coming out in my bathrobe, I rub my face with the make-up wipe until it glows.

My sister puts the make-up bag and rollers away in the bathroom She comes into the bedroom holding the tangled mess of black satin that I'd left on the floor.

"What sort of woman does that? I don't think I'll ever understand," she says, folding them carefully and placing them on the hanger.

"I don't know. I just don't know."

8

It Was Only One Time

"I wonder what happened to George?" Danny asks all of a sudden.

I look up sharply from my plate. "You mean George Haritzos?" For some reason my appetite vanishes. Swallowing a mouthful of wine, I like how it soothes my throat. "What made you think of him?"

"Dunno. I guess that song on the iPod. Remember? He used to play it."

"When was the last time you saw him?" Pete asks.

"I reckon about fifteen years ago." Danny cuts his steak. "After our wedding." He looks at me.

The three of us stop to listen to the Iggy Pop song and start our own journeys down memory lane.

"Yeah," Danny says. "It's like he's fallen off the face of the earth."

My wine glass is empty. I reach for the bottle and pour. "A bit more?"

Danny and Pete both nod.

"I saw him after he moved up to the Dandenongs. He was living like a hermit," Pete said, carefully placing his knife and fork across the plate to show he'd finished. He sat back in his chair and sipped the wine leaving a translucent trail sliding down the inside of the glass. "I reckon he's taken off interstate. Back then, he told me, he wanted to get away. He was a bit off the rails. He never said, but I reckon a chick broke his heart."

"It's funny how you grow up with someone and then drift apart. We should try to contact him, relive the old days," Danny says, draining his glass. "What do you reckon love?"

"Yeah," I say, "But maybe he's got his own reasons for cutting us off."

"Remember when he was playing in the band? He threw his guitar in the air and it got stuck on the rafters. I pissed myself laughing. I still remember the look on his face. He was trying so hard to be cool." Peter grabs a toothpick and digs around in his back teeth, looking satisfied when he brings out the dislodged hunk of grey meat.

Danny scrapes back his chair, goes into the lounge room and comes back with the iPad. I gather the dishes while Pete grabs another bottle of wine off the bench.

Danny hands me the iPad. "Look him up honey," he says, then adjusts the iPod playlist. A Nick Cave song comes on. George loved that song.

"Remember that time, when we went to the races for the first time. What were we? Eighteen?" Pete, holding the bottle starts laughing. "He was all dolled up in his bag of fruit and waited for us at the entrance to the members' enclosure."

Danny laughs too. "We were waiting at the other entrance for him. In those days there was no way to get in contact. He waited for an hour but we'd pissed off inside after ten minutes." Danny is holding the cheese platter on an angle; the cheese is beginning to slide. He stops laughing when he catches my stare. "I guess you had to be there."

I frown. "I was there, you idiot. It was our first date?"

Danny grimaces his apology. "So it was."

"The bastard had the last laugh though. He won over three hundred quid," Pete says.

I remembered meeting George that day. He was the cool hip type. He had a way of holding a cigarette just the right way. He'd been friends with all of us but I had my own memories which I wanted to ignore.

Still holding the iPad, I glance at the wall clock. "The game's going to start soon."

"There's plenty of time. See if you can find him on the internet," Danny says.

I type in George's name. "Nothing comes up." I'm relieved.

"Try another search engine; safari's shit," Pete says carefully cutting a square of cheese and placing it on a biscuit.

I search again. "There's nothing."

"Try the telephone book," Danny offers.

"There's two names with G Haritzos here. One in St Albans and the other in Sunshine," I say.

"Let's ring. He'll be one of them for sure," Pete says, whipping out his mobile phone after wiping his fingers on the napkin. I hand over the iPad and Pete dials a number. I chew on my nail and pray that no-one answers. But someone does. I clear the rest of the table and fill the dishwasher.

"Ah ... er Hello. I was wondering if George Haritzos is there please."

With my back to the boys, I slide the soapy cloth around the pan and hold my breath.

"Oh, I see. Thank you anyway."

I come back with the cloth and wipe the table.

Pete looks at our expectant faces. "Nup. He doesn't live there." Then he dials the second number and asks the same thing of the person who answers. He hangs up and shakes his head. "Not there either. She said she'd never heard of him. You'd think with a name like that he'd be easy to find."

"Maybe ... maybe he's dead," I say before sliding a strawberry across the cheese platter.

"We could search the death notices, except if he died a while ago it wouldn't come up on the internet," Danny says.

I check the time. "Come on. The game's about to start."

We take our wine and the rest of the platter into the lounge room.

"You know what? I'm going to try and find him.

At lunch time tomorrow I'll go to the Births, deaths and marriages and see what I can find out," Danny declares.

"Good idea," Pete says. "I want to find him too."

"Have we got any chips?" Danny asks. I sigh and get up to rummage in the cupboard.

*

The next night, when I get home from work, Danny's in the kitchen whistling and cooking up a stir-fry.

"How was your day?" he asks.

"Yeah, OK, I guess," I say, throwing my handbag across the back of the kitchen chair. I wrap my arms around Danny's waist and peek into the wok of sizzling vegetables he's cooking.

Danny turns and kisses me lightly. "I went to the Births, Deaths and Marriages today but I found nothing on George."

"Oh?" I say, pulling away.

"I can't understand it. How can anyone be anonymous in this day and age? He's not that old."

"It's possible that at forty-two he's not on the internet and maybe doesn't use technology," I say hopefully. "He hasn't bothered to contact us." I swing around and grab a couple of glasses, go the fridge for the white wine.

Danny's frowning. "Maybe we offended him. He had no-one after his parents died. You know, when we were growing up we were like brothers."

"Maybe Pete's right and he's moved on. Doesn't want to be found. It's pretty obvious that he doesn't want to be friends. Maybe he's left the country. People drift apart. It happens."

"That's it. He's gone to back to Greece. He moved here when he was young so he must have decided to go back." Danny scoops the stir-fry and the steaming rice into bowls and places them on the table. "He's probably got a nice Greek wife."

"And a couple of kids." I pour the wine and sniff at the food. "This looks good."

I hope he's let the whole thing rest.

*

A few months later, Pete, Danny and I are at the airport, waiting to board a plane to New Zealand. We're off to visit Pete's new girlfriend in Auckland. It's boring waiting so I decide to grab a coffee.

I sit at a table and thumb through an abandoned Herald Sun. The girl behind the counter calls out a name. I watch the suited figure walk across and take the coffee. I'd know him anywhere: his slender fingers holding the spoon and stirring in the sugar, the same broad shoulders. The girl calls my name. The guy turns and I freeze in my seat, unable to move, heartbeat thumping in my ears as I hold my breath.

"Sally?"

"George?" I stand up, hitching my bag over my shoulder.

He smiles. I remember the tangle of his long wavy hair, now cut short. I stare at those same brooding blue eyes and remember the taste of his lips on my tongue.

The girl behind the counter yells out my name again. It shifts me into action.

"You look well," he says.

I grab my coffee and take too big a sip, scalding my mouth.

"I'm well," I say. "You look just the same, except for the short hair. And the suit."

We stand awkwardly appraising each other, sipping our coffee. I notice the label on his briefcase says George Johnson. He follows my glance. "I changed my name."

Then we both start speaking at the same time.

"After you," he says.

"Oh I was ... I mean Danny and I were talking about you the other day. It's been a long time."

"Yeah. It has."

"We wondered where you'd got to. Pete even tried to find you in the phone book."

He shrugged. "It was better to cut myself off." He sipped his coffee and leaned his tall frame against the counter. I squirmed under his stare. "How is Danny ... and Pete?"

"They're good. Actually they're over there in the lounge waiting for me. We're going to New Zealand. Do you ... do you want come and say hello?"

He half turns and looks at them. I chew my lip and nervously wait for his answer.

"I don't think so," he says looking back at me. I hold my breath and want to tear away from his gaze.

"Danny doesn't know," I say throwing my cup in the bin. George nods his understanding.

"It was only one time," he says.

"Yes," I say suddenly remembering his hands sliding along my body and across my breasts.

"I'm very happy with Danny," I say.

"That's good." He drains his cup.

"I guess I better go."

"Yeah."

I turn and walk away and head toward Danny and Pete. Only I suddenly veer off to the ladies. I find myself a cubicle and slam the door shut. I try to breathe but gulp in the smell of fresh excrement. I vomit and feel better. Leaving the cubicle, I splash water on my face. The faint voice of a boarding call comes out of a loudspeaker. I walk out.

"Hurry up," Danny says. "Where the hell have you been? I've been looking everywhere for you."

"Oh," I say, "I didn't realise."

Danny grabs my hand and pulls me to the gate. I look back toward the café and swear that I can still see him standing there. Watching us, before we disappear down the tunnel. I look at my husband again and think it was only one time.

***

9

The Surprise

Mum was in hospital. But we could go and see her, Dad said.

I was surprised then, when she showed up at lunchtime calling my name.

"Charlie. Charlie," she sang out as I played on the school's cricket pitch. When I heard her voice, I leaped with joy. I'd missed her and here she was.

She beckoned me to the fence.

"Mum you're back."

"Yes, my love, and we're going on an adventure. Can you climb over?"

Of course I could climb. I was a master at it. I

could climb anything; trees were my specialty so a fence was easy.

She kissed and hugged me. "Mummy loves her little man." And I inhaled her. She squeezed me even tighter, so tight that I could hardly breathe, but I managed to wriggle out.

"Where are we going? What about my school bag?"

"We'll get it later. Have you had lunch?" she said, crouching down and smiling. I nodded. "Good then. I can't tell you where we're going. It'll spoil the surprise." She took my hand and I skipped alongside her down the street.

"Is Emma coming too?"

"No, my love, just you and me today."

I was even happier. My little sister was annoying. Then I remembered. The last time she told me I was getting a surprise, I ended up at the doctor who prodded and poked me. Then he jabbed me with a needle and took blood out of my arm. I tried not to cry but I couldn't help it. She was always taking me to the doctor and I hated it.

"Are we going to the doctor again?" I said looking up at her.

"No, darling. Not this time." She stopped then

and stooped down. She held my face like she was looking for something. "Not unless you're not feeling well. You do look flushed though." She felt my forehead. "Mm..."

"I'm alright. I just want to go on our adventure." That worked because she stood up, grabbed my hand and began walking. At long last, I had her all to myself and I was getting out of school. But then I remembered that it was going to be my turn to bat. I'd forgotten to say goodbye to all of my friends. Oh well I thought, I'll see them tomorrow.

I saw an acorn and kicked it along the path in front of Mum. She kicked it back with her fluffy slippered foot.

"Why do you still have your slippers on?" I said.

"My feet are tired."

"How can you have tired feet?"

"They just are," she said.

I kicked the acorn into the gutter and tried to reach for it but she held my hand firmly and pulled me back. "Leave it, Charlie."

"I'm thirsty," I said. But she ignored me. "Mum, where are we going? Can we get a drink? Can I have a milkshake with ice-cream?

She grunted and stopped.

"We've got to cross here. Now hold my hand tightly."

I skipped and jumped over the wide white stripes.

"Could I get a Nutella pancake?"

We stood at a set of lights waiting for the little man to turn green. The trucks whizzed by. Then we began crossing. I remembered Dad said we should never cross when the little man was red but here it was, still red. A truck beeped his horn and yelled, "Do you want to get yourself killed, lady?"

She stopped suddenly in the middle of the road. I looked up at her lovely face. She gazed into the distance as if she was thinking about something. She was always doing that at home. Sometimes I had to yell to get her attention. I looked past her.

"There's a truck coming," I said. "Mum, there's a truck," I yelled and pulled her along. This was probably a test. Sometimes she made me figure out when to cross so that if I was ever on my own I could cross safely. Except she usually asked me if I thought it was safe.

Then I saw the Pancake Parlour. Yes! I was going to get a chocolate milkshake and a Nutella pancake. As we crossed to the other side another truck beeped. I liked the sound that the truck horn made and tried to imitate it.

"Mum, mum, mum. Can't we go to Pancake Parlour? It's right there. Mum. Look. We can get a milkshake."

"After," was all she said.

"But mum, I'm getting hot. I'm thirsty," I whined. "When are we going to get there?"

She said nothing but kept on walking. We passed an old man who was pushing a funny chair. I badly wanted to climb up on it. Then we passed two men with pictures on their arms. I liked the colours. I thought I heard a school bell somewhere in the distance and wondered if it was from my school. Then Mum started to walk even faster.

"Hurry," she said.

She was walking so fast I was almost running alongside her. Her hand was sweaty in mine, but she never let go.

"Are we nearly there?" I said.

Then she stopped. She led me down a tunnel under the footpath and we came out on the other side of a railway track.

"Are we going on the train?" She nodded and let go of my hand. She seemed to be looking around for something. Then she began reading a poster on the wall. We were on the platform and I stood close to the edge and looked down the length of the platform and followed the track as far as I could see.

"Step back behind the yellow line son," a deep voice boomed. The voice belonged to a man with a uniform who strode passed and disappeared into the building.

"Come back here, love." Mum grabbed my hand. "Let's go."

"We're going on the train," I sang and skipped about. "Toot, toot."

We walked to the end of the platform and stood close to the yellow line.

I could see the train in the distance.

"Mummy loves you. Mummy loves you. Mummy loves you." She murmured over and over again. She held my hand so tight, it began to hurt. The train loomed closer and she stepped over the yellow line. I tried to yank her back, but she pulled me.

"Mum. The man said to stay behind the line." But she wasn't listening. She kept moving toward the edge of the platform murmuring mummy loves you, over and over.

"Mum!" I yelled and pulled as hard as I could. Didn't she know it was dangerous?

She was at the edge.

The train tooted again and again. I pulled again but she held me next to her like a vice.

"Mum! Stop! The train!"

It was almost upon us. She stepped forward.

Wrenching myself from her sweaty grip, I fell backwards, scraping my hand and arm on the hot asphalt.

I heard the squeal of the train's brakes; a man's frantic yell and a woman's scream.

The moment moved slowly. Then she was gone.

***

10

On The Side Of A Hill

The sun is low on the horizon when we stroll arm in arm around the large park. A mob of kangaroos stand tall, staring long and hard at us, ears twitching, dropping their heads to eat only after we're at a distance. We stop to take in the view. The bay spreads out before us shimmering flat except in the wake of an ocean liner, which sails in slow motion toward the Heads.

We pass a silent group of women, arms arched in Tai Chi moves. A flock of rosellas take flight. We stop to listen to rustling in the bushes nearby, hoping for a glimpse of something, which never reveals itself.

"The sign said this way," my husband announces.

But all we find is another lookout and more staring roos. The ocean liner edges closer to the Heads.

An old, dusty path leads us to a lake surrounded by reeds and a fence.

"There's another sign. Sculptures this way."

My enthusiasm and energy is waning as we climb another hill. I'm at the point where I want to go back, but we find ourselves in a picnic area, desolate except for a young couple on a chequered picnic rug.

"What a good idea?" I say. "Why didn't we think of doing that?"

He puts his hand against his forehead shading his eyes searching.

"They're probably celebrating their wedding anniversary," I say.

He glances at the couple before scanning the slope ahead.

"Nah. It's a first date for sure."

By now we've moved on and are on a path above the couple and can see what they see. The ocean liner is long gone. The sea is flat, its colour a pale blue.

"No, it's not. Look, they've got champagne and glasses and a picnic basket. She's not dressed up for a first date. Why don't we just sit on the grass and watch the sunset too? Let's forget about the sculptures. They're obviously not around here. I'm tired."

"Where's the map? I reckon we're close."

I rummage in my pocket, pull out the map and hand it to him. He studies it.

"I bet he's surprised her. They've been married a couple of years and he's gone to all that effort," I say. I imagine the man getting everything ready and telling his wife they're going for a drive. She would have smiled and kissed him.

I stare at the couple instead of the view. "You'd never think about doing something like that for me." The thought sneaks out and hangs between us. We walk on.

"What's that over there? Just past the pink barked gum. I think that must be one. See?" He points into the bush. "They're arguing anyway."

I swing my head back to gawk at the couple.

"Don't look!" he says. "Wow." My head swivels back to face the large sculpture ahead of us. "My god. This is magnificent," he says, studying the twists of shiny metal pretending to be art. "Your sister is really talented."

"How do you know they're arguing?"

"I heard them. Don't you think this piece is great? Look how the light reflects on the metal."

"What did you hear?"

His excitement drops and he sighs. "He told her to stop being paranoid. You should be checking out your sister's art. This is important."

I hear raised voices drifting away into the other direction.

"Stand against this tree and kiss me so I can see what's going on."

"I'm not going to do that. That's so obvious."

"Too scared to snog in public now?" I tease. "C'mon. At least stand there so I can face you and see what's going on behind you."

He complies but grumbles, "You're such a busy body."

Looking over his shoulder, I brush a leaf from his hair.

"I think you're right. Now he's pacing backwards and forwards."

He touches my arms and moves me aside. "There's another one. C'mon. Let's go."

"But don't you want to know what's going on?"

He grabs me around my waist pulling me into him.

"No. And neither should you. Stop spying on them. Now let's do what we set out to do."

"But what if that girl's in trouble? Maybe we should stick around."

"Now *you're* being paranoid. That's stupid. It's none of our business. She'll be fine. It seems to me you're chickening out." He grabs my hand and pulls me along. I know he's right but I don't want to go on. I turn for another look. The man is waving his arms as if in explanation. The woman, seated on the blanket, pulls her knees up under her.

We round the bend. More roos and a sculpture of a large shiny silver gnome.

I can't resist turning my head one more time, but the couple are no longer in sight. I'm torn. I want to see them and the fading view rather than face what I know is before me. He lets go of my hand and wanders ahead.

"There's meant to be another one further along the track," he calls out.

I stare at the gnome, but I'm thinking about the

couple. I'm agitated. My sister's sculpture disturbs me.

"You coming?" he calls out.

"Yeah." I jog to catch up and gasp. "Oh my god," is all I can say.

There it is: a skeleton of a small child lying in the bush. The title says, 'Lost'. The sculpture takes my breath away. My chest thumps and my hands sweat. For the first time in twenty years tears slide down my cheeks. I bury my head into my husband's shoulder and sob, the arguing couple and their woes replaced by a volcano of erupted grief. Slumped in his arms I'm comforted by my husband's smell and familiarity. After a while I pull away to stare again at the art piece.

"You alright?" he asks softly.

I nod and sniff. "It's more confronting than I expected."

"You said you were ready."

I wipe my nose with the back of my hand. "I thought I was."

He kisses me and holds me close. We stand together staring at it in the fading light.

"I thought I could handle it. All those years of counselling. Maybe I'll never get over it. Now that

I've seen this I don't know how my sister had the guts to do it."

"Maybe it's her way of dealing with the grief of losing her child."

I twist away to run up to the path. He catches up and we slow to a walk.

"I should have been watching out for her," I say. I try to control the tears but they come in a flood. "And… and none of us even noticed she was gone."

"You're being too hard on yourself. It was a long time ago. You were only a young girl."

He was right but it didn't make me feel any better.

"If only I'd checked on her."

"It wasn't your responsibility."

"You don't understand." I stare into my trusting husband's eyes and put both my hands on his arms. I have to tell him everything. "I promised my sister I'd check on her. That I was going to the bathroom, that I would go past her tent and look in." I wipe away my tears and gulp. "But I didn't check on her. I went behind the camping ground kitchen and smoked a joint with one of the boys." I'd finally said what I'd never said to anyone. What I'd tucked away. I wait for my husband to say something, but there's only sympathy and love in his eyes.

Then it hits me; I'd always had an excuse and now I know why. "I can't be trusted with kids," I blurt. "That's why... why we've never had any."

Turning away, I don't want to see the disappointment on his face. I'd failed us both. The realisation of why we had no children, the excuses and the lies, were out.

"I never told anyone... until now." I face him. "I'm really sorry."

He blinks and I can see he's trying to take it all in. Red marks multiplying across his neck show me his stress. I'm scared of what he'll do; what he'll say. I don't know if I can bare it.

"It's alright," is all he says. "It's going to be alright."

I wipe my eyes again and look into his face. But I can't make out what he's thinking.

"Do you want to go home now?" he asks softly.

I nod and sniff. We walk on in silence for a while, thoughts and feelings pummeling my core. We reach the front gate of our rented cottage.

"It's time," I say. "It's time I faced my sister again. Tell her what I did and that I'm sorry."

He kisses me and nods.

A swathe of orange cloud smears itself across the sky hiding the sinking sun.

"It's the right thing to do," he whispers.

***

11

The Holiday

The buzz of excitement quickly dies when we reach customs at Heathrow and have to line up like cattle, patiently waiting our turn to exit. With our passports and paperwork ready we say little to each other as we push our wheelie bags and shuffle along.

"Don't they know we're tired?" Judy says, voicing what we all think.

"God, look at that. Someone needs to tell her," Anna whispers. We follow her stare to the girl further along the line whose short black skirt is tucked into her undies. We each feel the need to save her from her ignorant humiliation, but she disappears in the queue.

"She probably doesn't care anyway," I say, leaning on one foot.

"This hair is driving me nuts," Judy mutters, trying to pat down her wayward red curls, tighter than old fashioned bed springs. A grey line zigzags along the top of her head. "I didn't get a chance to get a root job before we left. Is it that bad?"

"No, no. It's fine," we mutter and look elsewhere as we shuffle along.

Anna busies herself by scraping off the melted chocolate from her stylish blue slacks. She smiles at me through her perfectly glossed lips and pushes her dark hair behind her ears. How does she look so good with so little sleep?

Suze on the other hand looks as bad as I feel. She wipes the traces of mascara, which have smeared their way too far under her eyes, accentuating her already dark circles. I admire her bravery for leaving her hair to the ravages of old age, unlike me with my need to defy it at all costs.

I bob up and down on my toes, hoping the swelling in my ankles moves somewhere else. I try not to think of what I've left behind.

Eventually, we lumber onto a bus that promises to take us to the car hire depot. I lean against the grubby window pane and watch the expansive car park fly by as the bus meanders through the terminals, picking up more hapless travellers. I close my stinging eyes and try to relax my mind.

"Jackie! C'mon! Hurry up." Judy, already holding her overnight bag, taps my shoulder. I wake with a drop of spittle edging out of the side of my mouth.

"Huh. I'm coming," I say, slowly getting up to gather my belongings. Jumping off the bus, I spy my three friends already lugging their bags through the sliding doors ahead.

Breathing in the diesel fumes left by the disappearing bus, I sling my handbag across my shoulder and follow. Inside, Judy and Suze are manoeuvring their cases into the seating area at the end of the building. Anna is already waiting in line at the counter.

"Jackie. Over here!" Suze commands. "Put your bags there." Our four suitcases swallow up space for anyone else to sit.

"You guard the bags," Judy orders. "While Suze and I see what's going on."

I climb over a bag and fall into a seat. The narrow office fills up and I glare at anyone who glances at our temporary squat. The sun beams onto my shoulders and the warmth helps to relax me. I close my eyes and try to push away the turmoil in my head and heart.

"Excuse me. Do you think I could get past to sit down?"

"Ah. Err, sorry." I get up and move a bag aside just enough for the English toffee-nose to squeeze her spindly legs through. She sniffs as if there's a stink in the air and plonks herself onto the edge of the seat opposite. She clasps her oversized Louis Vuitton handbag to her flat stomach. I move the suitcase back into its place entrapping us both. Stretching my arms in the air, I discretely whiff. The deodorant is still holding out after thirty hours without a shower.

I try not to think about what was said in the car on the way to Tullamarine airport. Instead I look at the toffee-nose and wonder what her story is. Is she married? No wedding ring. Does she work? The look of her clothes tells me she's well off and I unconsciously judge her. She catches me staring, so I glance at my watch, which is still on Australian time, and concentrate on changing it.

"Right! We're ready to go," Anna says grabbing her suitcase.

Suze is right behind her. "I hope you understood the instructions about where the car is. I lost her when she said turn left at the sliding doors."

"I'm pretty sure I got it. C'mon. Let's get out of here. We've got an hour and half ahead of us," Anna says.

"Um. I have to go the toilet first," Judy announces.

"Me too. I'm busting," I say.

"Go on then. Hurry up," Anna groans. "I don't know why you two didn't go in the terminal."

She sounds like a mother hen which is pretty funny since she's never had any children. Still, we understand her. I forgive her climbing over me every hour in the plane to do her exercises. Deep vein thrombosis killed her sister a few years ago.

"Yeah. You're using up precious gin and tonic time," Suze smirks.

That gets us moving and I think about how much I need a drink while I finish up and hitch my jeans in the cubicle. When we come out, Anna and Suze are happily talking to the English toff lady as if they're old friends. I wipe my hands on my jeans, grab my suitcase and lead the way, for a change.

"So what did we get?" I ask.

"A Mercedes C Class station wagon," Suze announces proudly.

"There it is. Ooh, it's black," Judy says.

We abandon our cases and open the doors. The rich leather smell swirls around our nostrils and Suze caresses the seat. "It's beautiful."

"Let's get the bags in," Anna says, lifting the rear door. She looks at the boot then our cases. "Somehow we've got to get a hundred kilos of luggage in there."

We stand back and survey the situation, each trying to work the computations in our weary heads.

Suze, ever the impractical one, lifts a bag. "Let's put this one, this way and then yours on top." She grabs Anna's, which is the biggest. "Fuck! What the hell have you got in this thing. It weighs a ton."

"Hey. It's only twenty kilos," Anna says indignantly. "It's practically empty. There's lot of room for my purchases," she says cheekily.

Suze lays two bags next to each other, but they

still don't fit. My head begins to hurt and I can't offer any solution, so I just stand there in a muted daze, tiredness overwhelming me.

"How about this?" Judy exclaims. She stands the bags up next to each other then, pushes her bag in next to them. On top she throws three carry-on bags and slams the boot door quickly.

That jolts me. I'm standing there with my hands on my hips. "But haven't you forgotten just a tiny little thing? Like my bags?"

The others start laughing and Judy scratches her head and frowns.

"Easy!" she says brightening up. "Get in!"

I get into the back seat and Judy throws me my hand luggage. Then she slides my case into the middle and slams it up against me. She jumps in and the door closes, trapping us on either side of the suitcase partition.

"Good work," Anna says, as if she's just led one of her corporate team challenges.

We find our seat belts and click them into place. Anna starts the car. I get the iPod out and plug it into the car's speaker system. I think perhaps it's an omen when Bon Jovi's 'Living on a Prayer' blasts out.

Anna turns down the music. "Where are the gears?"

Suze, in the front seat, pretends to be busy trying to get the GPS to work. I begin to wonder if I should say something, as we all know Suze has little idea how to use a GPS, but I don't want to hurt her feelings.

"Aren't they next to the steering wheel?" I say, trying to sound helpful. "Any luck with the GPS?"

"Nup." Anna glances at Suze and looks for the gears. "Are there any instructions?" She fiddles with a lever and shifts it to neutral and then to drive. The car moves. "Here we go," she says gingerly steering the car out of the carpark.

"Thank Christ!" Judy exclaims. "I thought we were going to have to go back to that bloody office again. Do we know how to get out of the carpark?"

"Yep. She said to turn right, then right again at the roundabout, and then right onto the freeway. It's easy," Suze says, turning around and winking. "Isn't this exciting? I've been so looking forward to this holiday. And with my three best friends."

We each murmur our agreement.

I settle back in my seat, take a headache tablet and gulp down half a bottle of water.

Anna is driving too slow through the roundabout. A four-wheel drive is bearing down on the other side of us.

"Why can't I get the car to go above twenty?" Anna asks.

Suze looks up from fiddling with the GPS. "Just press the accelerator down."

Anna gives her a weak smile. "I am! It's flat on the floor and this is the fastest I can go."

We're almost at the entry to the freeway. Anna always knows what to do. She's calm in any crisis. But she's flustered now and I begin to worry.

"Quick! See if there's any instructions. It's like it's in some sort of cruise control. How the heck do I get out of it?"

Suze frantically rummages in the glovebox and finds a foolscap piece of paper. She looks at it upside down, then tosses it into the back seat to Judy.

"See if you can make any sense of it."

We merge onto the freeway and limp along at twenty. I peep back through the curtain of luggage – large trucks are heading straight for us before suddenly veering into the next lane.

"I wonder what the speed limit is?" Anna says quietly.

"I reckon it's faster than this," I volunteer from my backseat.

Judy is reading the instructions. "There's nothing about cruise control or speed."

"There must be something," Anna cries out as another truck honks us. Her knuckles have turned white on the steering wheel.

"I'll google the instructions," I offer, and open my iPad. "Oops. No coverage."

Anna groans and worry overcomes my weariness.

Suze resorts to pressing console buttons like a madwoman, and suddenly we take off. With the accelerator to the floor and traffic ahead, Anna slams on the brakes.

"Thank god. What did you do, Suze?" Anna's knuckles have gone back to their original colour and we're travelling at a normal speed.

Suze shrugs. "I have no idea. Just pressed one of these buttons. Maybe it was for the cruise control."

"Anyone notice the speed limit by any chance?" Anna asks again.

"Nuh," we chorus. But then we stalk the passing

roadside for it. Finally, a sign. Seventy! I rub my neck and try to relax.

"God, that's slow," Suze says.

"Yeah," Judy agrees.

"You nincompoops! It miles per hour not kilometres." Anna sits on the speed limit. "This drives like a dream. I'm in love with this car. I think I'll call him Daniel. He's the closest thing I'm ever going to get to a man."

We giggle.

"Don't worry. We'll stalk the English pubs until we find you a man," Judy says passing around a block of chocolate.

"They're overrated. You're doing fine on your own," Suze says.

I silently agree with Anna. We have rented a house in a small village in the Cotswolds. I couldn't imagine it teaming with men and especially ones that would be good enough for our Anna, who has always aimed too high. I think her corporate manner intimidates them, but I can't tell her that.

Gary Glitter is playing 'Leader of the Gang' and we're all singing along at the top of our voices. The chocolate kicks in and Suze, Judy and I are playing air guitar. A Fiat glides past and I glimpse a pimple faced teenage boy staring at us in horror. I can't resist poking my tongue out at him.

"So do we know where we're going?" Anna asks casually.

The GPS isn't working and no-one has internet. Then I remember the map attached to the email with directions to the house. "Are we on the M40?

"No idea," Suze says and turns Gary down.

"Yes," Anna retorts. "Didn't you see the sign when we entered the freeway?"

"I was too busy trying to get you out of your twenty-mile-per-hour cruising speed," Suze laughs. "That's going to be a great story to tell everyone." Judy and I giggle too, but Anna remains straight-faced. I don't feel so tired now.

"That piece of info has to stay under the cone of silence," Anna says, frowning.

"Don't be ridiculous. That's the first status on Facebook when we find internet," Judy says.

"We get off at Exit 22, turn left at a roundabout, and head west for twenty miles. When we see a red telephone box and a tall chestnut tree, we turn right. Does anyone know what a chestnut tree looks like?" I ask, glad to be helpful.

Judy grabs the paper I'm holding and studies it.

"What bloody stupid instructions? This isn't a car rally!"

"It's the best we've got," I retort, snatching the paper back.

"Don't worry. We'll find it. We've got lots of time," Anna says with a smile.

The lush green countryside spreads around us. Unfortunately, we've left the blue sky behind and clouds threaten.

"Do you know where the windscreen wipers are? I reckon it's going to rain," I say.

"NO," Anna and Suze exclaim in unison.

Anna presses a lever which fails to produce said wiper. A drop appears on the windscreen and the clouds grow darker. "Shit!"

"It's fine," Judy declares reading the instruction sheet. She peeks over her reading glasses. "It's a button on the console. It has a picture of a fan. Suze?"

"Here it is." Suze presses a button and the wipers come on just as the raindrops hit in a jumble on the windscreen.

"This is the stupidest car," Judy says. "What if you were driving by yourself. You can't just fiddle with the levers and buttons, hoping for the best."

"Leave Daniel alone. I should have familiarised myself with him before we left," Anna says smiling. "Look the rain's stopped. There's blue sky ahead." She flicks the button.

"What time is it in Melbourne?" I ask, looking at my watch which has decided to stop.

"It's tomorrow," Judy says, giggling.

"I wonder what everyone's doing?" I say.

"You're not feeling homesick already?" Suze asks. "I know you've never been away from Dave and the girls, but it's not like they're babies. They can look after themselves. They're in their twenties for god's sake. And you need this holiday. We all need it."

She's right. So, how do I tell them that after thirty years Dave wants a divorce? That the Dave they know is a man who has had a mistress for ten years? And that my world came crashing down when he told me on the way to the airport just over thirty hours ago? And he will have moved out by the time I get back? Gutless wonder! After all I've done for him. Raised his children, worked in the business, supported him when he decided to go back to Uni. For what? For nothing. This is the sort of thing that happens to other people. Not to me, I want to scream. "Yeah, I know. I was just thinking about them, that's all." I reach into my handbag to grab a tissue and compose myself.

"I'm so glad you said yes." When Suze smiles, it hides the fear she has for her teenage grandson who has tried to commit suicide. She told us of her worries during the flight. I wonder how she copes on her own. Then I remember and wonder how I'll cope. Suddenly, my chest tightens with panic and I want to be home again.

"Yeah, wasn't it lucky we could all come?" Anna says.

"It's going to be an adventure." Suze turns up the music and I turn off my problems and join in to sing along to 'Walking on Sunshine' by Katrina and the Waves.

Anna turns the music down. "Isn't this the prettiest countryside? So green. Such a change from dry brown paddocks."

The green hills speed by and I think about how the drought has drained us. We're all looking forward to running a shower for more than two minutes at a time. I look at Judy sitting across from me and wonder at her strength to carry on and rebuild after the bushfires two years ago. I know what she'll say when I tell her my news. She'll be sympathetic, but she'll tell me to brush myself off and get on with life. Just like her. That's what she did after Max died.

"Does anyone want to stop? After all that water, I need a pee and a snack," I say. "According to my stomach it's way past dinner time, if we were back home." In truth, I just want to get out of the car, to get clean air and space and not to feel as if I'm in some sort of dream.

"Cross your legs," Suze laughs, throwing a half-full chip packet at me. Jokingly, I mouth something foul at her. The girls haven't noticed anything's amiss and I'm glad. I have to think, even though I don't want to.

"Good idea. I'm getting a bit of a headache. Let's get some lunch. How about there?" Anna points to a roadhouse marked with a food, toilet and shopping sign. Three miles on, she veers off the freeway and guides Daniel to a stop in a large carpark. "I know we don't need petrol yet but we might as well find where the button is for that."

We spill out of the car. I yawn, stretching my arms and body back into an arch. Walking around to Judy's side, all I see is Anna's ample bum in the air. Her head is somewhere under the steering wheel. She pops out and her round face has turned a deep crimson from the exertion. "Can't find the petrol button. Where's that bloody useless sheet?"

Judy dives into the car and jumps up waving it in the air. She scans the sheet. "Surprise! There's nothing about petrol on this."

Suze gets back into the car and presses buttons. Up pops the boot. She gets out of the car laughing. "I've tried everything. At least we can pop the boot now."

"What about pressing the petrol door thing," I say. "That's how I open mine at home."

"This is a luxury car with lots of security and state of the art bits in it," Judy lectures. Her teacher self can't help it. "It would have to have some sort of button. I know, did you check the glove box?" The girls are standing around arguing the merits of the security system and the mod cons, which none of us know anything about, when I press the petrol door and it opens.

"Ah um ... ladies. The petrol has been solved. Now let's get inside. I'm starving and in dire need of a wee."

We're in a happy mood. Even me. Here we are,

friends for years, on our first overseas trip together, for two whole weeks. Even tiredness can't dampen our spirits. We're free from our worries and cares of husbands, children, grandchildren and elderly parents.

With hot English tea quenching our thirst we chat excitedly about what we're going to see and do. Judy wanders off in her colourful happy-pants, bought on her last trip to Bali, and comes back with three bulging shopping bags.

"I bought a few things for tonight. There's actually a huge supermarket here. This place is amazing. Some nibbles to go with the gin and tonics we got at the airport, and fish and salad for dinner. Oh and some chocolate for dessert."

It was amazing what she's found in a place we thought only served a cup of tea, a few staples and petrol.

"You know, there's even a hotel here. Can you believe it?" Judy says. "Why would you want to stay here in the middle of nowhere, forty-five minutes from London?"

We shrugged and look around the food court of what seems to be a two-storey shopping mall. We glimpse clothing shops on the level above us.

"Should we go and check it out?" Suze asks applying lipstick expertly without the help of a mirror.

Anna glances at her watch. "I'm tempted, but it's nearly two thirty. We've got another forty-five minutes at least before we get to the Cotswolds. Let's get out of here while I still have the energy to drive."

We murmur our agreement as we gather our things. Weariness has set in and we trudge out to the car. The wind has picked up and the sky threatens rain. I pull my cardigan around me, crossing my arms to keep warm. The groceries thrown into the back, we settle into our seats. I'm looking forward to closing my eyes in the comfort of the back seat, that is until I'm called on to find the chestnut tree. But my thoughts swirl. I'm angry thinking about all the things I should have said to him.

"Are you still alright to drive?" Suze asks.

Anna smiles and nods. "I'm fine now I've had a cup of tea. We're not too far away." Anna starts the car. A red light blinkers on her screen and something beeps with annoying insistence.

"What now?" she says.

"Someone's door is still open," Suze says.

We open then slam our respective doors.

"Gee, it's gotten cold," I say. "I should have put my scarf on. My neck's cold."

"Oh, haven't you got a seat warmer like us?" Suzie turns around and she and Anna giggle.

"What?" Judy and I shake our heads.

"I want a refund," Judy murmurs, throwing her coat over her shoulders.

Anna moves the car forward gingerly but the light continues its impatient warning. Suddenly, Suze jumps out of the car and runs to the back to slam down the boot and the beep stops. We cheer as she gets back in and Anna moves towards the exit, only to stop behind a line of cars.

"Let's get some music on." I start the iPod and 'The Joker and the Thief' blares out. The four of us are bobbing our heads and the car is rocking. A truck in front obscures what's happening ahead. We're happy singing at the tops of our lungs and it helps me to forget. It feels good to let go. Dave would have frowned and told me how embarrassing I was. A few people walking to their cars stare then look away. The song finishes and Anna turns down the volume.

"Something must have happened on the freeway. We're certainly not going anywhere fast." Anna is clicking her French manicured nails on the steering wheel in time to a song I can barely hear. We've moved five metres. The rain starts to fall and the pain returns. Trying to pinpoint when our love died, I realise I'm not as distraught as I should be. I wonder when I should tell my friends. Anna will take it badly; she always wanted what I'd had. She'll offer legal and financial advice. Suze, who introduced Dave and me, will be angry with him. They'll listen. They'll offer suggestions, but am I ready for what they'll say?

"Hey, there's an old person in a wheelchair going faster than us." Suze giggles. "No wonder they have a hotel here: their own version of 'Hotel California'. Jackie, you're awfully quiet. Are you ok?"

"Yep. Just tired." But I worry the cracks are appearing.

We chat quietly to pass the time and try not to stress as Anna inches the car forward a foot at a time. We move fifteen metres in fifty minutes. Silence. Trapped. In the rain. We can't go forward and we can't go back.

"Ladies!" Suze pipes up. "That tea is going right

through me. Do you think you'll still be here if I duck into the toilets again?"

I suddenly need to go too. "I'll come with you."

We get out and run. Somewhere, between the cars and the entrance, tears spill out and join the raindrops on my face.

"You look like a drowned rat." Suze's hair hangs limp and wet down her shoulders; black mascara streaks her cheeks. And then I laugh uncontrollably, as if expelling the pain of the last couple of days.

And she laughs hard too. We must have looked a sight. Cackling and crying, wet and bedraggled.

"Stop!" Suze gasps. "I'm going to pee my pants." Then she runs to the toilets.

Now composed and feeling weak, but somehow lighter, I follow more slowly. It's quiet in the food court. Everything seems slow. People sit with cups of tea and stare at . . . me, at Suze, at the rain and each other. I shiver and quicken my pace.

After we finish, Suze grabs another packet of chips on the way out. We shake our heads. Daniel has moved three car lengths. The line of cars snakes around the carpark and out onto the freeway ramp. Everything is at a standstill.

We get in, dry ourselves off as best we can, settle back to enjoy England to the sounds of Cilla Black, and munch on salty potato chips. Cars ahead of us begin to move. And I know then, I'll be alright.

***

12

A Reason To Get Up

Wheeled in after my surgery, I hear Doris before I see her.

"There's no need to fuss," a raspy voice says. The nurse tucking in the sides of the bed ignores her. After she leaves, Doris untucks the sheets, pulls back the covers and grumbles.

Stifling a smile, I pick up a magazine, but can't concentrate. Sitting opposite Doris, I see everything she does. Her wispy dark hair has a white stripe down the middle of her head, her wrinkled lips stretch smooth when she talks. The lines across her face don't give me a clue about what life she's lived, but watching her distracts me from my own pain and misery.

We've been thrown together in this two bed ward.

"I owned my own employment agency and I can tell you, dearie, that you're in the wrong job. Nurses are meant to be caring and that's not you. I tell you this for your own good. If I want to go and do exercise, then I will. Right now, I have to do the crossword."

The pain stops me from moving and I'm uncomfortable. I settle back and smile at the nurse who peers at me. Is this the same nurse the old lady was talking to?

"How are you feeling Bec?" She pulls the curtains around me before I have a chance to take in my surroundings.

"OK," I mumble.

"Any pain?" She whips out the blood pressure cuff and fastens it around my arm.

"A little." I wince.

"OK. Let me see." Removing the cuff, she writes something on the chart. "You can have more pain killers. I'll sort that out for you. You should feel more comfortable very soon."

"Thanks," I say weakly.

Gentle kisses on my cheek wake me and the big brown adoring eyes of my small daughter stare into my face.

"Did I wake her?" She looks up at her father who smiles.

"How are you feeling?" Paul says.

"Yeah. OK, I think. A bit uncomfortable. How's my baby girl?" Emily's black hair is tied in a ponytail on the side of her head.

"Mummy, I missed you." She tries to climb up to give me a kiss.

"Hold on a sec, darling, while Mummy gets comfy."

"Emily. You can't sit on Mummy. She's sore."

"But I want to."

"It's OK. Darling, sit here next to me."

Emily settles herself and I put my arm around her and notice Doris is dozing.

"Mummy. Why is she snoring?" Emily shouts. She smells of chocolate and there's a smear on her dress and on the side of her mouth. She can't help it but she wriggles.

"Shh, Emily. The lady's trying to sleep," Paul whispers.

"What's that thing on her face?" Emily whispers loudly. She swings her leg against me and I wince. She's nudging herself as close as she can to hug me.

"It's a mole that special people have," I say. "What did you have for lunch? Was it chocolate?"

"How did you know?" Emily asks incredulously.

"Mummy's know all sorts of things. Paul?" I signal to him that I'm in pain and he lifts Emily off the bed and holds her.

"I had a chocolate ice cream. Daddy's going to take me to the park. Can you come too?"

"When I leave the hospital and when I feel better. I will come and swing you so high that you'll fly in the sky."

"OK then. We better let Mummy rest now and go to the park," Paul says, putting Emily down "Do you want anything?" He gives me a quick peck.

"Can you bring me a book? I forgot to pack one."

"Which one?"

"Climbing the Coconut Tree. It's on my bedside table."

"What do you think you're doing?" Doris snarls.

Jerking my head away from Paul, I see that Emily has snuck over and climbed onto Doris's bed. Her outstretched hand is caught in Doris' vice-like grip. "I want to touch the mole," she says.

"Emily!" In three long strides, Paul has reached Doris who lets Emily go. "Emily. That's naughty." To Doris, "I'm so sorry."

"I'm really sorry about that," I yell out from my side of the room. "She's my daughter."

I catch her glare just before Paul picks up Emily. "Let's go to the park and we'll see Mummy tomorrow. Blow kisses to Mummy."

"Bye, Mummy," Emily says, pressing her chubby hands to her mouth and then out in a wave. "Love you, Mummy." And then they're gone. My daughters' declaration of unconditional love gets me every time. And I sniff. Trying to sit up, the reminder of why I'm here plunges me into sadness. I'm hungry but nauseous at the same time. No amount of painkiller has removed the dull throb. I want to be out of here. Holding hands with Emily and Paul, eating chocolate ice cream in the park.

"What's her name?" the raspy smoker's voice interrupts me from feeling sorry for myself.

I wipe my eyes. "Emily."

"Pretty name. Had an aunt who had that name. She's was a bitch though. That the father?"

I nod.

"So moles are for special people, heh?"

"Oh, sorry we disturbed you."

I can't read her to see if she's offended. And I don't get a chance to say anymore. A flotilla of medical staff comes rolling in and heads straight for Doris. One nurse briskly swishes the curtains around them as if it's a cone of silence, but it only makes me want to listen.

"Doris, you don't mind if I have some med students with me do you?"

Mumble, mumble, mumble.

I'm disappointed. The wall of curtain actually seems to work and I settle down to read a magazine.

The cover sports one of the Kardashians but I can't keep up as to which one. It seems to me there's one on every cover of every gossip magazine. They bore me senseless. I flick through and my attention is caught by an image of Turia Pitt the woman who was burned while running a marathon in a bushfire. I'm inspired and fascinated and settle down to read.

"Listen young man. I owned my own employment agency. I'll have you know I ran it for thirty-five years and found employment for fifteen thousand, three hundred and nine people. But if you don't watch out ..."

I glance across at the curtain. What could have got the old girl so worked up, I wonder. All I hear is the low rumble of a male voice, followed by the imploring tone of a female, all of which are suddenly drowned out by the noise of a machine in the hallway.

I doze off and when I wake, find a plateful of sandwiches and a cup of tea in front of me. The magazine has been placed neatly on the side table, along with my water. I suddenly realise I'm hungry and down the ham and cheese sandwich. Chewing, I meet Doris' staring eyes.

She's rolling the food around in her mouth. I smile. Doris continues to stare. I notice a line of cheese and biscuit packets in front of her. She sweeps them into her lap. I blink and wonder why she has so many.

"Nice lunch?" I ask.

"If you like pig slop," she grumbles. "They don't like me here," she says.

"They're just doing their job," I say righteously.

"I asked for sandwiches like you, but all I got was this swill disguised as soup."

"What about all that cheese you've got there?"

"What cheese?" she says. "You're seeing things. They got you on too many drugs. You just watch these people. You think you come in here to get fixed up but they don't fix you. They slowly make you worse. You know why?"

"I don't agree. They want you better and out to free up the bed for the next person." I'm beginning to think she's the one on too much medication.

"It's so they get more money from the government. Every day I'm here, they get more money." She winks and nods. "You mark my words."

For someone who thinks the soup is swill, she makes a lot of noise slurping it. The skin under her chin wobbles like a turkey as she swallows. My appetite vanishes. Pushing the table away, I lower my bed and settle against the pillows. I'm suddenly very tired.

I doze on and off. Someone removes my lunch.

"You know I used to own an employment agency. I could have got you a better job than this," I hear her say. I smile, then doze again.

I only wake when the nurse comes in. I'm curtained off from Doris and the nurse is busy doing something to the drip.

"How's the pain?" she asks quietly.

"Uh. OK." I try to sit up. "What time is it?"

Apart from the light in the hallway and the lamp next to me, the room is in darkness.

"It's four in the morning."

I'm surprised. I've slept through dinner. I'm not hungry, but I'm still sleepy. The nurse switches the light off and I settle back into the pillows. Doris is snoring. She reaches a crescendo then stops as if she's holding her breath. She lets go and snores up to another crescendo. I'm restless and the drip in my arm bothers me. I lie awake thinking about Emily. Hoping she's sleeping through and isn't fretting as much for me as I am for her. I wonder how I'll stop myself from spoiling her, now that she's an only child. I rub my stomach but the ache is still there.

I hear the cleaners before I see them. The beginning of the day shines through the large window, and as the room fills with light, I notice the view. The gardens are sprawled below, their yellow, orange and brown leaves signalling the summer heats' brutal end. I'm glad. The heat and pain wore me down.

"Your kiddy coming in today?" Doris is sitting up, staring at me again.

"Yes, probably."

"Nice." Is all she says when breakfast arrives.

"The view is beautiful from here," I say.

Doris ignores me. She busy examining everything on her tray. "Where's me cheese and biscuits?" she asks.

"It is breakfast, Madam," the orderly says with an accent. "You will get at morning tea time."

The orderly has a pretty face and I smile my thank you when she places my tray before me. She responds by turning away abruptly.

Eggs, toast, tea, banana and, cheese and biscuits. I wonder about the cheese and biscuits as I enjoy the eggs.

After breakfast, the doctor arrives and examines my wound declaring that it's healing nicely. The catheter and drip come out, releasing me from my bonds. I'm told that I will be getting up and going for a little walk today. I'm pleased with the plan.

I get off the bed. I feel woozy but proud to get

to the bathroom unassisted. While I'm in there, I think about why I've never seen Doris out of bed.

Shuffling back, I pick up the cheese and biscuits and head toward Doris.

"I couldn't help overhearing you before. Would you like to have my cheese and biscuits?"

Doris stares at me, rolling her food around her mouth like a cow. She waves her hand before swallowing.

"That's very nice of you. Thanks. Put it on the side table there if you wouldn't mind."

I get close. Doris is busy peeling the banana and picking off the brown bits. The drawer is slightly ajar and I can't help noticing that it's full of cheese and biscuits.

I open my mouth to say something but think better of it.

"You know I once owned an employment agency. I could get you a job if you like."

I look around the room thinking she's talking to someone else, but she looks directly at me with blue-grey eyes, sunken in folds of skin.

"Oh, did you? How long ago?" I gingerly walk back to my own bed and sit.

"It was a while ago. I found jobs for twenty-five thousand people."

A gum-chewing physio with a high, flying ponytail breezes in.

"Hello. My name is Tania. It's time to start you on physio. How about I help you out of bed so you can come to class today?"

Tania looks enthusiastically from me to Doris.

"Who?" I say.

"Why both of you." Tania says.

"I'll come," I say.

"Doris?" asks Tania.

"Nah. I'm too busy."

"Come on, Doris. You need to get out of bed. Otherwise, your muscles will forget what to do. Let me help you."

I push myself off the bed and wait. Tania holds out her hand to Doris, ready to help her out of bed. Doris ignores the hand and crosses her arms casting a lofty scowl.

"Clean your ears out, missy. I'm not coming. Do you know I used to own an employment agency? You're in the wrong job."

Her hand hung in space, Tania's face turns red.

"OK. If that's what you want, Doris." She rolls

her eyes skywards and moves to my side "Let me help you." She holds my arm gently and leads me out of the room.

When we're out of earshot, I ask, "Why doesn't she want to go?"

"Dunno. She never wants to get out of bed. We've tried everything. Reckons she can't walk. That's why she's in here: getting tests. But she can still get into a wheelchair. She's in and out of here all the time. Between you and me, I think she likes the company. It's like a holiday for her."

The exercise group is fun. Tania puts everyone at ease and cracks a joke, which makes me hurt when I laugh.

I'm allowed to go back to my bed on my own. I pass the morning tea trolley. My stomach rumbles and I feel pretty good.

As I walk into my room, I wonder why the curtains are drawn around Doris's bed as well as mine. Walking toward my bed, I notice Doris through a crack in the curtain which hasn't quite made it around my bed. Standing next to my bedside table, she's pinching the cheese and biscuits from my tray. I slip back through the doorway into the corridor and peek from my hiding spot. She walks back to her bed without a sign of difficulty.

I lean against the wall in the corridor, watching the bustle of busy people, and wait until I think Doris is back in bed before re-entering our room. The curtains are drawn back on both beds and my tray with its cup of tea is waiting. There's no sign of the biscuits.

Sipping my tea, it's my turn to stare at Doris. She smiles back innocently, stirring the sugar in her teacup. I look down at my tray and notice the absence of sugar.

"Is your kiddy coming in today?"

"Yes," I say. "She'll be here soon. She's got kinder this afternoon. What about you, Doris? Are you having any visitors today?"

She squints over her teacup as if she doesn't understand the question. She puts her cup down. "Did you know that I used to own an employment agency?"

"Yes. I did know that. You mentioned it already. Where was the employment agency? Here in Melbourne?" I sip my tea.

"Actually, it was in New York City. I lived and loved there."

That set my cup down. "Is that right? Where did you live?"

"Manhattan of course. I was married to a very nice man and I made him very rich."

"How long ago?"

"A long time ago."

"Mummy, Mummy." My daughter's voice and footsteps echo down the corridor. I'd know her anywhere.

She comes bounding in wearing jeans and a checked shirt I haven't seen before. Pauls' attempt at buying her clothes makes me smile.

He's holding a bag and flowers.

"How's my girl?" I ask.

"Mummy, look what I brung you!"

"Look what I brought you," I correct, taking the large drawing thrust into my hands. "Did you do this? All by yourself?"

"Yes. See that says, I love you," she says proudly. "Daddy helped me. Do you like it?"

"I love it." I'm conscious of Doris's stare. She sits looking forlorn and lost, holding her wrinkled hands in her lap. She catches my eye and turns to look out of the window.

Paul unpacks the bag he's brought, then goes off to look for a vase.

Emily wanders over to Doris.

"Hello," Doris says. "Would you like a biscuit?"

Emily nods. Doris goes into her drawer and pulls out a packet of cheese and biscuits and hands it to Emily who runs back to me.

"Say thank you to Doris," I coax.

"Thank you," Emily says at the top of her voice.

Paul comes back in with a vase full of flowers and leans across to kiss me full on my lips. He tastes of coffee and I yearn to be home. He picks up Emily who is trying to climb onto the bed and sits her next to me.

"What have you got there?" he says.

"Biscuits. That lady gave them to me."

Doris is smiling at Emily. I wonder how long those biscuits have been sitting in the drawer and want to tell Paul to take them off her, but I can't.

"Daddy. You open?"

"Darling. Why don't you have them later? After lunch," I squeeze her and plant a kiss on the side of her chubby cheeks.

I talk quietly to Paul about what the doctor said while Emily hugs me. But she soon gets restless as she decides to jump on the bed. Doris is watching and listening. And I feel guilty. She looks sad and alone.

I snatch off a flower from my bunch and give it to Emily and whisper to her.

Emily takes the flower and walks over to Doris. She holds the flower up to Doris who takes it and beams. I quickly whisper to Paul about the biscuits while Doris is distracted.

Emily and Doris are chatting quietly and the change in Doris is remarkable, almost youthful.

It's then that I decide.

"Help me up, Paul."

"Emily and Doris. How would you two like to go for a walk? Emily can you help Doris?"

Doris smiles at Emily who holds out her hand.

"Come, Doris, to the park?" Emily pleads.

Paul and I stand next to them while, remarkably, Doris gets out of bed.

"Quick! Help Doris put her slippers on," I whisper to Paul who looks quizzical but does what I ask.

Doris and Emily are deep in discussion. About what, I don't know. But what I do know, is Doris

is shuffling along, holding Emily's hand and that's
reason enough to get up.

***

13

I've Got News

I'm sorting the roses into height and colour when Damien bursts into the kitchen. He's flushed and his arms are laden with bags of groceries which he plonks on the bench. Tins of tomatoes spill out and one tin lands in the middle of the roses.

"Hey! Watch where you're putting that." I retrieve a pink rose and carefully examine it like a newborn baby. Irritated by his lack of consideration, I open my mouth to say something, but Damien has already disappeared. Before long, his footsteps thump heavily back into the house. I quickly move the roses to the sink before he plonks another load of bags on the remaining counter space.

"Whew! It's bloody hot out there," he says, slumping into the kitchen chair and throwing his car keys on the table. Usually he walks, but today he must have come back to get the car to pick up his purchases. "Can you make me a cup of tea, love?"

I survey the bags of groceries strewn across the kitchen and flip the jug's switch. The roses lie waiting for me to build my display, but I'm already resigned to searching for space for twenty tins of tomatoes.

"Bargain were they?" I say, holding up a tin.

"Yeah," he says, stripping off his socks and shoes. The smell of sweat and wet wool filters across the room. "A dollar a can. I couldn't pass it by?" He grins, oblivious of my mood. "They'll come in handy."

"In a snowstorm, which we'll never get," I say. I can't help but laugh at his misplaced enthusiasm. "Do I need to remind you that we live in Melbourne and it's summer? Those stinking stocks already tell us that."

He picks up the socks and sniffs them. "Ugh.

They're bad alright. By the way, I've got some news."

I'm on the step ladder straightening the cans in lines of three on the top shelf of the pantry. "Oh yeah. What have you found out this time?" Retirement to him means coming home from his daily walks with bits of useless information and groceries we don't always need. Yesterday, he found out three shops had closed down in the nearby shopping centre, so he bought five steak knives for $2. The day before that he ran into someone he knew and found out their eldest child had moved out. Last week, he chatted to the people in the house opposite and discovered they were selling and moving to Canada.

"I'll get rid of these. I need a cup of tea first and then I'll tell you." His expression is serious as he wanders off to throw the shoes and socks onto the veranda. The kettle whistles. I step off the ladder and pour bubbling water over teabags in two cups. A bug has escaped from one of the roses and I flick it into the sink. Pouring the remaining boiled water on it, I watch the bug writhe, then disappear into the plughole.

"No wonder you take so long," I call out. "You

spend more time picking up gossip and groceries than walking." After pouring the milk, I place the teacups on the kitchen table then turn and grab the twenty-four-roll packet of toilet paper and throw it to Damien as he returns to the kitchen. He heads off to the laundry, while I stare into the pantry, trying to work out where I'm going to put the rest of his groceries. I pick up a packet of saffron and stare at it.

"Walking an hour a day is good for me," he says padding to the kitchen bench. "I've lost two kilos so far."

"What did you get this for? We're never going to use it." I scan the docket. "Fifteen dollars for that!"

He slouches at the table and blows to cool his tea. "It lasts for years. It'll be good for paella," he says sheepishly.

"We've already got some," I say, rummaging in the cupboard and pulling out two packets of the stuff. "For goodness sake, when you go out, take the list and stick to it. You're spending a fortune."

He ignores me and sips his tea. "Forget about that. Now sit down. I've got some really important news." He's frowning and I'm fearful that I'm not going to like what he's about to say.

"Alright." He waits while I sit down and pick up my cup. "Mary Dunlop has passed away."

I put the teacup down.

"Oh my god. What happened?"

"Suicide." His chocolate brown eyes search my face.

"What? That can't be right. She wouldn't have done that."

"I know. I can't believe it either. It's true."

"How?"

Damien shrugs. "Jackie didn't say."

Jackie is Mary's daughter.

"When did it happen?"

"Nearly a week ago. The funeral is next Wednesday. Jackie was coming out of the shop when I bumped into her. I gave her our condolences and offered to help. But she said she was fine."

"Yes, yes. Of course." I get up and begin pacing. Mary was an old friend. Our children had grown up with hers. We'd been very close once, but we'd drifted apart after the children had grown and gone their separate ways. "Did Jackie say anything else?"

"Nuh. She was in a hurry."

"Poor Pete. He must be devastated. We should ring him."

Damien nodded. "Yes. I'll do it."

"Why didn't he let us know?"

"Dunno. Guess he didn't want the questions."

"I saw Mary not long ago." I look at the calendar and punch the date with my finger. "It was two months ago. She seemed fine. This doesn't make sense. Why would she kill herself?" I sit again, head in my hands. "Oh this is so terrible." Tears fill my eyes. "Why didn't she tell me she needed help? Why didn't I pick it up?"

"It's not your fault, love. I saw her too. Only a couple of weeks ago. She came into the bakery when I was getting the bread rolls. She said she'd call to make a time to catch up and go out for dinner."

"Making plans to go out for dinner doesn't sound like a woman who wants to kill herself."

I pick up my mobile phone and press a number on my contact list.

"What are you doing? I said I'd ring him."

"Hello. I'd like to order a box of flowers please."

Damien nods his head in understanding.

We pull into the carpark of our local Anglican church. People are streaming in. Sally, our youngest, has flown in from Hobart.

"There's Mack," I say. "And Alice." Their children, Harry and Freya, are walking on either side of them.

We hurry to catch up. They'd known Mary and Pete for as long we had. Our children were all the same age. After the obligatory hugs, Alice and I walk together with the men and children trailing behind.

"I just can't believe it," Alice says to me, blowing her nose. "Such a shock."

I nod and entwine my arm with hers. Her black patent leather shoes shine in the bright sunshine. "I know. Did you have any idea?"

Alice looks at me.

"That she might have been suffering from depression?" I add. I've decided that it's only depression that can drive a person to suicide.

"No idea. She always seemed fine. But then I haven't seen her for months. Mack played golf with Pete only a few weeks ago. He didn't let on there was anything wrong. Although he did mention they were going to sell the house."

"God. That house was her pride and joy."

"I know. Mack said he saw it listed and then it went off the market." Alice whispers. "Mack reckons Pete was in trouble. Played the markets too hard."

More people we know mill around the door of the church and after greetings, we find a seat. I scan a sea of solemn faces, some familiar. Damien reaches for my hand and squeezes it. I crane to see if I can see Jackie or her sister, Emily, or their father. But all I see is their mothers casket, covered in red roses: her favourite colour and flower.

She and I started our rose gardens more than twenty years ago, when Jackie and Sally were at kinder. We shared cuttings with each other. She had a green thumb, her roses bigger and more perfumed than mine. I couldn't help but feel I should have been a better friend. I wonder at her despair, and what it must have been like inside the home she loved. And the energy she would have needed to keep up the appearance of the happy, vivacious woman we all knew.

The service starts with a prayer and a hymn. Then Pete's bald head bobs up and he walks to the microphone. He speaks as if he's giving a speech to his shareholders. He reminds us that Mary had come from England at the age of seventeen, that she'd gone to Melbourne University and studied Art and History before taking a job as a curator in a gallery, which had closed more than twenty years ago. Then he sits down. Nothing about raising his children, nothing about their life together and his love for her?

"That's it?" I whisper to Damien who quizzically raises his eyebrows. I don't hear the drone of the Minister. I ponder the eulogy given by her husband of thirty years. He'd been almost cold and detached. Perhaps he's still in shock. But something in his blank face doesn't make me think so.

"He's not sitting with the kids," Damien whispers. I crane my neck and see that his two children are one side of the aisle, but he has walked to the far end of the pew on the opposite side.

Next to speak is Mary's brother.

"He must have flown out from England," Alice whispers to me. She hasn't removed her sunglasses, but I can tell from her red nose and sniffling, like mine, her eyes are a mess.

Mary's brother, in stark contrast to her husband,

breaks down. I'm astonished to learn things that I didn't know about my friend. That she was fluent in four languages, having lived in France, Germany and Spain as a child. That a painting she did when she was younger hangs in The Louvre and that she turned her back on her talent to follow Pete, the man she fell in love with. He manages to talk about her beautiful heart and her goodness, her love for her family and garden, her work with those less fortunate and her support for Pete and his business empire. She never complained when his business interests took him away from her for weeks at a time.

Alice's crying eggs me on and together, along with everyone else, we sob. We cry for Mary's children whose mother's love has gone. We cry for the unborn grandchildren who will never know her and her sweetness. But most of all, we cry for ourselves – for not caring enough to be there for her, when she needed us.

The service ends and the casket is carried by Mary's brother, husband and other men I've never seen before. I try to study Pete's face as he comes towards us but others block my view and, too quickly, he disappears.

"Beautiful service," someone says. Was it beautiful? I wonder. None of us should have been there. Mary should have been out and about enjoying the sunshine, the singing of the birds and her glorious roses.

We slowly shuffle out and head around the corner to the hall where we're told refreshments will be served. I glance at the hearse and the polished bare box inside where my friend now lies. Pete is being hugged by someone but his face is still devoid of emotion. I wait and when it's my turn, I smile weakly and all I can say is a pathetic, "I'm so sorry for your loss, Pete."

"Thanks," he says, letting me go so that another person can step in to take my place.

"Are you OK, Mum?" Sally puts her arm around me and gives me a hug. "It's so very sad," she says. "I feel so sorry for Jacks and Em. It must be awful. I couldn't bear to lose my mother." My eyes fill with fresh tears as I feel my daughter's lips brush my cheeks.

I rush to the bathroom to pull myself together. In the cubicle, I hear others come in. Taps turn on and off. The dryer roars with hot air.

"Can you believe that eulogy? Heartless bastard.

Why did he even bother? He threatened to sell her house from under her, so he could get the cash to set up a new house with his latest floozy."

"No! Are you sure?"

"Yep. She told me herself. I can't believe he had the gall to bring her today."

"But why didn't she take him for all he's got? She would have got millions."

I don't hear the rest. With elbows on my knees and head in my hands I sit and cry again.

Finally, I come out. Swollen red eyes, streaked mascara and smudged foundation greet me in the mirror. After splashing myself with cold water, I unzip my make-up bag and go to work on fixing the mess. Looking presentable enough, I sigh, before sliding into the crowded hall. I scan the room. My daughter is chatting animatedly with old school friends. Groups of women with cups of tea stand talking. One slips off her high heel and flexes her foot. Jackie carries a plate of food to an elderly woman who is seated on a chair and talking to Em. Pete is nowhere to be seen.

A hand touches my shoulder and I'm relieved to see Damien holding out a cup of tea.

"OK?" he asks. "Thought you'd be hanging out for this."

I take the cup and gulping too quickly the hot liquid scalds the back of my dry throat, bringing more tears to my eyes. "Ooh. Too hot."

"Take it easy love."

"Thanks. I feel drained. It's been so much more emotional than I expected."

"I know. Come on, we better mingle." Someone waves Damien over and I join a group of women I've known for years. There's Donna who's married to the CEO of a listed company, and Liz whose husband left her for another man. Together with Mary, Susan and Jane, we made a formidable team on the primary school council. The six of us ran the fetes, the cakes stalls and were the social hub of the school. Like Mary and I, we drifted when the kids went to different high schools.

"Now he can't sell the house, can he? He put it into her name for the business. She told me years ago, it was to help avoid tax," Susan says. Susan is a country girl but has lived more than twenty years in the suburbs. Her husband has MS and she supports her family as a nurse.

"I told her she should have dumped him ages

ago," says Jane. "But she said the debts were too big. I told her to see my lawyer. She'd have unravelled it all for her. But she'd signed everything he told her to. Never bothered reading what she signed. That's one thing I learnt, a long time ago with hubby number one. Never sign anything unless you've seen a lawyer." Flipping her long, bleached blonde hair, Jane looks smug. She's up to husband number three, living in a large house in Brighton. She's kept old age at bay with plastic surgery and Botox and, according to Sally, her children despise her.

"Isn't it all a bit odd?" Four sets of eyes stare at me.

"What do you mean odd?" Susan says.

"Don't you think that her suicide is odd? Why would she do it?" I ask. "I'm trying to understand. Did any of you have any idea that she'd do this?"

"Well ... no. But I suppose his womanising has pushed her to it. You can't blame her can you?" Jane says.

"What womanising?" I ask. "Am I the last to know? Is this common knowledge?"

Susan snorts. "Where have you been? He's tried it on all of us in the past."

The others murmur and I'm embarrassed. "I had no idea."

"You're not his type. No offence," Susan says. Her lipstick has made a rim of red around her cup. "Mary knew of course. She just turned a blind eye."

"That's probably why he didn't sit with the girls," Donna pipes up.

"Why didn't any of us know she was so desperate that she couldn't see a way out? I don't understand why she would leave the children and grandchildren that she loved more than anything in the world. Susan did you know? Jane, did you?"

"Ah, er … no," Jane says.

"Do any of you know what actually happened? Was there a note? Have any of you spoken to Emily or Jackie?"

"Well, no. They've kept it very quiet. It's painful for them. We can't just bowl up and say, '*Hey Jackie, Emily, tell us how your mother topped herself. Do you know why she did it?*' Get real. This is a funeral for god's sake," Jane says. "What about you? Have you spoken to them?"

"We're all hurting," Susan says, patting me on the arm. "It's hard for all of us." The others murmur into their teacups and I wander off to put my empty cup on the table. I realise how much I hate these mindless shallow women and wonder if maybe Mary did too. Maybe she hated us all.

In the car on the way home, Sally blurts out, "I spoke to Jackie."

"Did you?" I swing myself around.

"Apparently there was big row. Jackie didn't know until her mother told her the next day. Her father asked for a divorce. She said she was very upset."

"Well, Mary would be," I say.

"Not her, Mum. Jackie! Jackie was very upset."

"Oh, yes of course she would be."

"Then she met her dad's new girlfriend. Did you see her? She was the blonde one. She looked younger than me."

"Yeah, I saw her. Big boobs, short skirt," Damien says.

"Dad!"

"Oh. I didn't see her. How's Jackie coping?" I ask.

"She's not too good. I'm going over tomorrow to see her . . . you know, take her out for coffee. Mum, Mary didn't even leave a note. She never gave Jackie or Emily any reason. How could she have done that? Wouldn't she have thought about them? What about Emily's little girl? She did it days before her only granddaughter's second birthday. Did you know that?"

"I had no idea."

"And did you know that Em is expecting another baby?"

"Oh god. Poor Emily."

"Why do that to her daughters, Mum? Why?"

I shake my aching head because I don't know what to say. I have no answers.

"The whole thing is very strange," Damien finally says, pulling into our driveway. "Maybe the coroner's report will reveal more."

"What? What are you talking about?" I ask. We trudge into the house.

"When someone suicides, there's usually an autopsy and the coroner gets involved," Damien explains. "He must have released the body for the funeral." He pulls at his tie throwing it over his head and onto our bed.

"You don't think something fishy is going on?" I'm dumbfounded.

"I dunno. I'm just saying what happens. The police will be involved. That's all."

Sally has followed us into our bedroom. "Maybe Jackie's dad murdered her mum. Think about it. He wants a divorce. She says no, then a few weeks later, she's dead."

"Don't be ridiculous. Go and put the kettle on," Damien says. "Pete would never do something like that. I've known him for thirty years, I should know."

"But how do you really know, Damien? How do any of us really know what happens behind closed doors? No-one shares that."

"I just know."

"Or maybe Pete's girlfriend did it," Sally calls out.

I throw my heels in the corner and follow my daughter into the kitchen while Damien changes.

"Maybe you've hit on something, Sally. They were saying he had financial difficulties. That he wanted to sell the house. Susan said the house is in Mary's name. Maybe she refused. Maybe she stayed with him because she feared him."

Each of us absorbs the possibilities.

"I think we're getting ahead of ourselves. I'm

sure if there was anything untoward the police would be onto it," Damien says, padding into the kitchen in bare feet.

He pulls out a pot. "Tuna pasta? I've got plenty of tuna and loads of cans of tomatoes."

"Sounds good, Dad." Sally is reading something on her mobile phone. "I'm going out for drinks at seven. Will it be ready before then?"

"Yep. We don't see you for weeks on end and you're not going to spend any time with your poor old parents?" Damien smiles and Sally gives him a playful punch on the arm.

"I'm here now, Dad. Enjoy."

I leave them and go into the lounge where I sip my tea and try to watch the news, but the thoughts jumble around in my head. I want to blame Pete. It's his fault that Mary's dead. Even if he killed her by his own hand there's no denying my friend died from his betrayal. Blaming him pushes away responsibility for my own neglect of a friendship I'd allowed to lapse.

*

Weeks pass and everything is back to normal. Damien goes out again without the list and brings home another load of shopping. This time he's found twenty tins of lentils and chick peas.

"They were on special. Fifty cents a can. You can't go past it. By the way I've got some news." He puts the shopping on the floured bench I'd readied to roll out scones. I'm cooking them for an afternoon tea I'm attending later.

"Damien. Stop. Didn't you see the flour? Now it's everywhere."

"Sorry, love." He rescues the bags and spreads their floured bottoms on the kitchen table instead. "This is big news."

"What then?" I carefully cut the scones and place them into the tray.

"You'll never guess."

"What? I'm in a hurry." I push the tray into the oven. "Tell me."

I look at him and he has a smug look on his face. "You were right."

"About what?" I swiftly clean the bench and gather the bowls of jam and whipped cream. "Hurry up and tell me while I'm changing. I'm running late."

"The police arrested Pete this morning."

"Oh my God." I sit heavily on the bed and my guilt ebbs away. "That certainly is news."

***

14

Out of Nowhere

Eddie concentrates on the long road ahead. The dry flat countryside is dotted with gum trees and the odd windmill. There's little traffic, but his hands are tight on the wheel.

"You humiliated me again."

Here we go, Eddie thinks, not even half an hour into the drive home and she starts.

"No, I didn't. You did it to yourself," he snaps, before realising he should have kept his mouth shut.

He glances at his wife, but her face is turned away. He knows she's crying. When his eyes return to the road there's a ute with a trailer of wood in front of him and he wonders where it came from.

"I'm sick of it. You never want to do anything. I organised this weekend away so we could do something together." She sniffs, then reaches for a tissue in her handbag and blows her nose.

He unconsciously checks his mirrors and speed, and automatically lifts his right foot slightly. "And we did. I did what you wanted didn't I? I went away with you. How much did it cost by the way?"

"The cost is not the point. I paid for it. What do you care anyway? It's not like you put your hand in your pocket," she hisses.

He feels her eyes boring into him but he concentrates on the trailer ahead. It's swaying behind the ute.

"You know I don't like that airy fairy shit," he presses. "And I sure as hell don't like that new age crap they dished out for us to eat."

"They made a lot of sense if you'd bothered to listen and open your mind to it. But no, you had to start heckling and ask stupid questions."

"God spare me. It's a load of shit." He rolls his eyes as he remembers the argument with one of the facilitators. They were supposed to wear Lycra to perform yoga moves. He wasn't going to have a bar of it. He couldn't even get his leg into the pants they were given, let alone his burgeoning belly. No alcohol and no meat. What the hell is a man supposed to do? It was one of the worst weekends of his life.

"It's not shit. It's important to me. To us."

She always has to have the last word, he thinks. He blames her new friend, April, with her spikey hair, hairy legs and new age ideas. He didn't like it one bit. The lentil burgers, the incense and yoga had gradually crept into their house. Then the meditating? He didn't get it. It was just breathing to him. The first time he tried it, he opened his eyes and stared at the group. His stifled snigger had him ejected from the room. He probably shouldn't have called everyone wankers as he left.

In truth he'd rather have gone to the footy with his mates than go to a health spa. It was his own fault. He hadn't been listening when she told him about the weekend. He thought they were going to a resort. He'd consoled himself that he could watch the footy and have a few quiet ones while she went off and did whatever she did at the day spa.

He reaches across and turns on the radio . . . to

SEN: his favourite station. "Collingwood has hit the front!" the announcer exclaims. He strains to listen for the score. Why can't she come to the footy? He'd asked her enough times. When they were first going out, he'd bought her a season membership. She came every week then. But after they were married, she made excuses. She dragged him to art house films; the sub-titles were a drag. The ones with tits and bums were alright. Then the art galleries. She was always trying to improve him. Maybe she was ashamed of him. He hadn't thought of that before. He did an honest day's work. Sure, he wasn't a big wig with his own company, like her. But someone has to dig holes and fix the roads. Beside he likes being outdoors. She'd liked that about him.

His wife stretches her perfectly manicured hand and snaps off the radio. In the early days he'd loved to hold her hand in his, to kiss the tips of her fingers, one by one. Then he'd work his way up her arm to her neck and her full lips, kissing her and sliding his hands over her. He couldn't get enough. Now he's just annoyed that he missed the score.

The trailer veers dangerously across the double

lines. He slows to create more distance between them.

"I don't think you're in the least bit interested in me."

He sighs. "Oh yeah? I never take interest when you cart me off to your work functions. I never drop everything to listen to you when you've had a rough day at work. Yeah, I'm a real arsehole."

In truth, he adored and worshipped his wife, but he'd stopped telling her. And now she was too busy finding fault with him. Why didn't he clean the dirt from under his nails? Why did he leave his shoes and overalls in their white bathroom? The washing machine doesn't work – as if he'd broken it. Don't put your feet on the couch. He remembered when she loved to have sex on that couch. Now it was hardly ever.

"I've tried really hard. But I just can't anymore." Her voice cracks and she blows her nose again.

"For Christ's sake." A large roundabout looms. The ute slips through but he slams on the brakes to give way to a white Holden and a silver Mazda coming through on the right. He snatches a look but she's gazing out of the side window.

He accelerates and follows the vehicles as if in convoy.

"What the hell are you talking about?"

"I just can't."

"Can't what? Can't sit there arguing with me? Can't stop making me feel guilty for every goddam thing I do?" He looks at her again. "What?"

She meets his eyes before turning to stare out of the window again. He notices the setting sun, the windmill, the sheep grazing without a care in the world.

Her pain confuses him as he concentrates on driving. He knows he's above the speed limit but he's keeping up with the convoy. He also thinks he knows what she's talking about. But then sometimes it's like she's talking another language.

"I . . . I don't think I can be married to you anymore," she says quietly. She's no longer angry and he hears her sniff.

"Fuck!" he says.

The ute suddenly veers and swerves to miss a kangaroo that's come out of nowhere. He takes his foot off the accelerator.

"I'm sorry. I've tried ... but I have to be with someone who gives me what I need."

"Jesus!" he says.

He can't ask her what she means. He can't ask her about the fleeting thought that maybe there's someone else. And he can't say what he wants to. His eyes are locked onto the cars ahead. The trailer has separated from the ute. It's airborne. The Holden swerves to miss it and skids to the other side of the road, narrowly missing a truck coming the other way. The Mazda in front careens into the trailer and they spin and twist together like dancers, heading straight for them.

He grips the wheel, slams on the brakes and hears her screams. In that small moment, he wonders where he went wrong.

***

15

The Robbery

It's funny how we remember where we were and what we were doing during the big moments in our lives. The ones that are forever etched in our minds and dragged out at unexpected times.

Like when Diana died in 1997. The morning after a wonderful overnight stay in the city, I arrived home to relieve my mother-in-law, Grace, of babysitting duties. The day was overcast and cool, not unusual for August in Melbourne. Twenty minutes later, Grace rang to say someone had broken into her home while she'd been staying at mine. With two kids in the car, I was on the freeway on my way to Grace's house, when I heard the news for the first time on the radio. There'd been an accident and Diana was injured. The headline held me. I remember thinking, from the words the announcer used, that it wasn't that bad.

Arriving at Grace's, my focus shifted to her. The house ransacked, a window broken and stuff strewn everywhere. Questioned by the kids, I grappled to explain to them what a burglary meant. Could it happen to us they asked? The rise and fall of their anxiety required all my energy to calm them, and my mother-in-law. Dealing with the police who were in autopilot – questions, writing, bland expressions reflecting a run of the mill problem – somehow steadied me. It wasn't a big deal. I wanted to take Grace's mind off the fact that someone had rifled through her draws, invaded her sanctity and peace of mind. But it unnerved us all. What if Grace had been home alone? With my own husband, Michael, away, what if this happened to me? My euphoria of partying from the night before completely disappeared.

Then I remembered Diana. But Grace's television had been stolen and I didn't own a mobile phone. I wanted an update. News about her was better than what I had in front of me.

"Make a list of everything that was stolen for the insurance company," the well-built twenty-something policeman said.

"Will the robber come back?" My nine-year-old daughter Sarah frowned with concern when she asked him.

"Probably not," he said kindly. Then to my mother-in-law, "They might revisit once you've replaced everything. They know what you have now." Writing something on his clipboard, he missed the look of horror and fear across the faces of my mother-in-law and the kids.

"Mummy, will the robber come to our house too?" my six-year-old daughter Lily whimpered. I scowled at the policeman imploring him not to educate us with statistics. But he was already on the move to examine the broken window.

"No, darling. Not at all. He doesn't know where we live." I don't know why it came out. It was stupid. Home burglary was usually random. I knew that. But it satisfied her. "Why don't you both go out and see if you can pick some flowers for grandma's table?"

The other policeman who looked to be in his thirties smiled at me. Did he understand my stupid response? Did he have kids too? I glanced at the gleaming wedding ring on his finger – mine looked dull in comparison.

"We notice that the garage window is also broken. Have you checked the garage?"

"Oh, that window was already broken. A branch fell on it a few years ago and my husband was going to fix it but ..." Grace choked on the words.

I rushed to her side, put my arm around her and pulled her close. The tissues I'd stuffed in my pocket for my hay fever came in handy for both of us.

"He passed away not long after the window broke," I explained.

"Sit down, Grace," I said. "I'll make a cup of tea. Officers, would either of you like a cup of tea or coffee?"

"No thanks."

I left Grace slumped on the couch dabbing her eyes with the twenty-something policeman sitting next to her.

"Are you OK to give me some details?" I heard him ask. "A bloke is coming to dust the window for fingerprints. Then you can arrange for it to be fixed. It shouldn't be too much longer."

"Yes, thank you," she sniffed.

Filling the kettle, I watched the kids through the kitchen window. They were chasing a butterfly around the backyard. Their worry had been fleeting, while mine was still anchored. How will Grace feel about sleeping here tonight, all alone? Should I offer to stay until Michael gets back from his business trip? I'd dropped him at the airport this morning, before picking up the kids. I looked at my watch. He'd still be in the air. I'd have to wait at least until this evening before getting him at his hotel. I wondered if he'd heard about Diana before he boarded.

I rummaged in the cupboards for the tin of biscuits. Lifting the lid, I released the aroma of dark chocolate and peppermint. Picking two, I took them outside.

"Girls, come and get a biscuit!"

They ran to me, their arms outstretched, pretending to be airplanes. They swooped past, plucking the biscuit from my hand then ran to the back of the garden.

"Where are the flowers?" I called out.

"They're coming, Mum," Sarah replied.

"We're planes flying high in the sky to see where

the best flowers are for Grandma's table," Lily explained, swooping by me again, bits of biscuit spilling from her full mouth.

I tried the door to the garage and stepped inside. It was as it had been. The old curtain flapped from the chilled air squeezing through the splintered cracks of the grimy glass. Dust had settled thickly on the workbench and the scattered tools. A creeper had wound its way through a concrete roof tile and around a dark wooden beam. Cold seeped from the cracked concrete floor through to my thin shoes and into my feet. Dry, rust-brown splatters were still smeared on the sides of the bench, but the rest had been washed away from the floor. I sneezed twice to expel mildew. Nothing had been touched since my father-in-law had fallen here, the electric saw still going in his hand. I wondered if Grace had ever stepped foot in here since that day. Whether she had made peace with herself for having been only metres away in the house, while he lay here for hours. Dying.

"Mum! Mum. Where are you?" Sarah voice pierced my ears. Shivering, I glanced around for one last time and spied the radio. Should I get a news update on Diana? But Sarah's nagging call pulled me out and I closed the door behind me.

"Yes, what is it?" The words came out sharper than I intended.

"Can we have another biscuit? Please?" she pleaded.

"Please? Mamma, please." Lily's occasional lisp hung in the air.

"Only one more," I said, pulling my cardigan around me. "Stay here."

Setting a plate with several biscuits I took two more outside before taking the tea into the lounge room.

Grace looked lost in the big armchair. It was as if I was seeing her for the first time: her tired eyes peering through their dark circles as she took the steaming cup with shaking hands. I offered her and the policemen a biscuit, but I was the only taker.

"It's cold in here. Do you mind if I put the heater on?" I asked.

Grace nodded but her attention was on the older policeman.

"I'm worried that he might come back," she said. "Could he return?"

"Highly unlikely," he said. "Perhaps you could have someone stay with you tonight?"

He glanced at me.

"Of course. I'm happy to stay with the girls or you could come back to my place?"

She looked doubtful.

"It's better to help her settle if she does stays here tonight ... ideally with someone here," he explained to me. "Then you might like to get deadlocks on the doors and windows. It's always good to make it as hard as possible for the perpetrator."

This is not like falling off a bike where you have to get back on immediately, I thought. Was he a psychologist now? I was irritable. The plans for today had already been dashed, not that I could remember what else I was going to do, apart from clean the house. Still, what right did he have to give advice? And why was I angry at him instead of the burglar? Or Michael. He should be here dealing with this, not me.

But all I did was nod agreeably and answer the door when the bell sounded.

A man in blue overalls stood there holding a bag. "Ah, err, hello. I'm here to do the fingerprinting."

I stepped back onto the shoe of the older policeman who had crept up behind me.

"G'day Steve. This way, mate."

He showed Steve to the broken window while I joined Grace in the lounge.

"Just the fingerprint guy."

She nodded. We could hear the murmured voices of the three policemen. The room was growing warm from the wall heater's blast. Grace's face was flushed.

"Why did this happen to me?" she whispered.

"It's not you. It was just an opportunity. That's all." What did I know? I had never been robbed. "It's probably some young kid on drugs looking to get his hands on anything he can sell quickly. Chances are he won't even remember where he's been."

There was hope in her sad eyes. "Do you really think so?"

"Yes, I do." I thumped my empty cup onto the coffee table. "This is your home and you deserve to feel safe. Now, I'm going to call a glazier to come and fix the window and the locksmith to change the locks. Then I'll duck home for some clothes and we'll stay for a couple of days with you."

"Thanks, love. I don't know what I'd do without you. But I feel a bit guilty about pulling the girls from their beds and their routine."

"They'll think it's fun. And anyway, Michael won't be back for a few days. It'll be company for me too."

Her grateful smile made me forget my own selfishness.

The police eventually left and the clean-up started as, outside, the heavy clouds burst. The girls arranged the flowers on the table then sat down to draw a picture each to pin to the fridge.

Sweeping the glass and the invasion away as best we could, I told Grace about Diana. She clasped a withered hand to her mouth. Tears sprouted and the emotion of the day spilled out.

"That poor woman," she said. "Hasn't she had enough? I pray she's alright." Of course we both knew of Diana's problems: her husband's infidelity, her growing boys, the divorce, her work with children, the gossiped affairs. It was the soap opera of the nineties hitting the front pages of our papers, dominating the news and our lives, as if Diana were a part of it.

Then Grace gasped from her bedroom – her

grandmothers priceless diamond ring was gone. It had been earmarked for Sarah. An emerald and ruby engagement ring for Lily was also missing.

I left the girls and went home. Flipping between radio stations to get news, all I got was inane music for the ten minutes it took to get home. Grabbing clothes for us all and a portable television, I jumped in the car. While I stopped to give way on the freeway on-ramp, a song by the Spice Girls was cut off with the announcement that Diana was dead. It was only the beep of a car horn behind me that made me move. I don't remember the rest of the drive. I wiped the tears away as I walked through the front door and told Grace.

The glazier arrived soon after. "Have you heard the news?" he said.

"Yes," I said. "It's just too awful."

*

Now, here I am, ten years later, with Grace in a home, Michael living with another woman and both daughters overseas. And all I can think of, as I see my own shattered kitchen window, is where I was the day Diana died.

***

16

Lucky

I always thought I was lucky until the day I found myself lying on the floor screaming.

It wasn't luck like winning the lotto luck but I'd had a charmed and easy life. Coming along after five other children, my mother often remarked that I was a nice surprise. She used to say it was lucky for me that there were five other siblings to do all the chores. All I did was sit on my doting father's knee and suck my thumb while my brothers and sisters grumbled and worked.

I received a lot of attention from everyone in the family. There was nothing I could do wrong and when it looked like I could get into trouble for something, all I needed to do was fill my big blue eyes with tears, and pout. No-one had the heart to chastise me, even though breaking the antique vase, when I was nine, was probably my fault.

I adored my brother, Peter and my sister, Betsy. They taught me how to do my shoelaces. They fought about who would hold my hand and take me into my first day of school. They made sure that my other brother, Joe and my two other sisters, Molly and Becky looked after me even though I don't think they really ever warmed to me much.

My earliest memories were of my siblings fighting each other; something about getting the blame for writing their names on the wall in the lounge room. I wasn't paying too much attention to them. I had just learnt how to spell everyone's name, and was practicing with crayon on the smooth white surface under the table. I guess they weren't too happy, but they told me I was lucky.

When I reached my teenage years Peter and Betsy left school and soon after, home. Betsy let me stay over at her house with her new husband. She cooked the most incredible apple pies and sewed me a gown for my first dance. She was so proud of how I looked especially after she did my hair and makeup. She declared, "I really don't know where you get your beautiful blonde hair and lovely clear skin. You really are lucky."

My parents both had black hair, olive skin and dark brown eyes and the rest of my siblings followed suit. A throw back from our Swedish side, my mother once said.

By the time I dated boys, no-one really cared too much about chaperones. My older sisters said I was lucky they forged the way for me. Perhaps my parents were just too old to bother. So I was free to do whatever I liked.

As for school, I was very popular. My figure blossomed and I was always the centre of attention. Of course it wasn't without a substantial amount of work. Sitting for half an hour while my sister brushed my long hair one hundred times required patience, another of my attributes. Girls wanted to be like me, and boys wanted me to like them. Betsy said I was so lucky.

My father died of a heart attack and my mother passed away soon after – everyone said it was a broken heart, but I always felt it was something more. I missed them, and maybe caring for my mother in her final months had something to do with my choice of career.

Passing all of my subjects, I decided on nursing as a profession. I know that probably sounds odd, given that most people couldn't see me looking after anyone other than myself. But, I surprised everyone. I was good at calming patients and many asked for me in the ward when I was on duty. I guess I just had a knack.

One day in the hospital ward, I introduced myself to an old man, Arnold who'd suffered a stroke. His eyes widened; I guess he was frightened by the loss of his ability to speak. Could you imagine never being able to talk? With both arms broken when he fell, all he could do was grunt; and grunt he did. Constantly. It bothered the other patients in the ward so much he had to be moved into his own room. But still he wouldn't stop. I would catch him staring at me and grunting.

"There, there Arnold," I would say to him, "You may be able to speak soon." I'm not sure why I spoke in a baby voice but it seemed to soothe him. But again and again, he would try. It seemed he really had something very important to say. So I sat with him and stroked his hand until he calmed and fell asleep. In fact, I was the only one who could keep him calm, so I saw a lot of him.

"Where's your family?" I said one day. "Do you have someone I can call for you?"

But all he could do was look at me with his big sunken eyes and grunt.

It was several days before they could find his son. I was holding Arnold's hand and taking his blood pressure when he came bursting into the room.

"Dad!" he exclaimed hugging him. "I had no idea. I got back this morning. Are you alright?"

I slipped away to give them some privacy. After a while, the son wandered out of the room with a worried look.

"Excuse me nurse," he said. "I'm Sam Ferguson. I've only just got back into the country this morning. I need to talk to someone about my father's condition."

"Of course," I said. "I'm Lily Franklin, your fathers nurse. If you'd like to stay with your Dad, I'll arrange for the doctor to come and speak to you."

There was something about Arnold's son. He was tall and good looking. His left hand was bare of jewellery and when he looked at me I melted. I couldn't believe my luck. I decided then, I'd met my future husband.

I asked to do more shifts just so that I could nurse Arnold and see his son. His mother, he told me, had died giving birth to him and his father had raised him on his own. And, of course, Sam quickly fell in love with me. We tried to keep it a secret; stole fervent kisses on the hospital grounds during my break. He often waited for me after my shift and I took him back to my flat. We had so much in common that he sometimes finished my sentences. I instinctively knew what he thought. He loved chocolate chip ice-cream and so did I. His favourite colour was blue as was mine. I had known no love like it before.

The days passed and Arnold improved and he was eventually moved so I saw little of him. Sam communicated to his father by writing questions on a pad. Arnold would nod or shake his head.

Sam and I were inseparable. I introduced him to my family. It was important to me that Betsy and Pete liked the man I loved.

Then, when we were out to dinner, Sam proposed. A violin player stood close to our table and Sam knelt on one knee, held my hand in his and asked me to marry him. I said yes, of course, and immediately smothered him in kisses.

The ring was spectacular; the diamond the biggest I'd ever seen. I couldn't stop admiring it and my fiancé. I was so lucky.

It was time to tell Arnold, who by this time was in rehab. Sam told me he still grunted a lot but had made slow progress but at least his broken arms were almost healed. Sam gave him the board with paper and a marker pen attached so that his father might practice. He was doing well Sam said. His father would learn to write eventually, but it would be perhaps years, for his speech to return. To get about he used a walker which he pushed out into the garden and back again.

It had been weeks since I'd seen Arnold and I was excited to visit him with Sam. I'd grown fond of my future father-in-law. Flaunting our love for the first time we held hands, when we entered his room. He was sitting up in his bed, slowly eating his lunch.

"Dad," Sam said. "You remember Lily. She nursed you when you first had your stroke."

I flashed him a smile. He stared at me and stopped eating.

"We've been seeing other for a while and well, we wanted you to be the first to know. We're going to get married."

Arnold dropped his fork on his plate and spluttered.

"What's wrong dad?"

He grunted and waved his arms around frantically. Why was he so agitated?

"Dad?"

"Here!" I said, grabbing his board. "Tell us what's wrong?"

Arnold held the marker pen in his fist and slowly scrawled the words, 'No! Is your sister.'

All I could think as I fell to the ground screaming, was that my luck had run out.

***

Acknowledgements

As always there are many inspirational people to thank for their help and guidance in bringing these short stories together. To Peter Lingard, who carefully read and critiqued each story, providing encouragement and humour along the way. To Nicole Hayes and my friends at Phoenix Park Writers group, who workshopped each story and provided valuable feedback, support and encouragement – I couldn't have done it without you. To Annie Collins who gave me her editorial expertise. To Robert New and the Monash Writers Group who provided me with encouragement and support throughout the writing and publishing process. A big thank you to Douglas Goudie and

Valerie Hudson for their advice and feedback during the proof reading process.

A special thank you to Con, who produced the artwork especially for the cover. His unwavering support and love know no end. Georgia and Eva – thank you for listening, for your support and feedback.

Each story in the collection represents something special to me and while it is a work of fiction, I was inspired by real life stories, the characters around me and the simple things that happen in life which can leave a lasting mark.

"The Surprise" was shortlisted for the Lane Cove Literary Awards in 2016. "On the Side of a Hill" was published in the Monash Writers Group Anthology in 2016 and is reproduced in this collection.

About the Author

After many years in corporate life, S.C Karakaltsas accidently reinvented herself by learning how to write. Unravelling letters written in 1948 by her father, she began writing an historical fiction novel in 2014 and finished up with her debut novel, *Climbing the Coconut Tree* published in 2016. She is currently working on another historical fiction.

She lives in Melbourne, Australia with her husband, two daughters and elderly cat.

Say hello at sckarakaltsas.wordpress.com or tweet@skarakaltsas

Other Books

Climbing the Coconut Tree

Inspired by true events, this is a story about eighteen-year-old Bluey Guthrie who, in 1948 leaves his family to take the job of a lifetime on a remote island in the Central Pacific. Bill and Isobel, seasoned ex-pats help Bluey fit in to a privileged world of parties, dances and sport.

However, the underbelly of island life soon draws him in. Bluey struggles to understand the horrors left behind after the Japanese occupation, the rising fear of communism, and the appalling conditions of the Native and Chinese workers. All this is overseen by the white Colonial power brutalising the land for Phosphate: the new gold.

Isobel has her own demons and watches as Bill

battles to keep growing unrest at bay. Drinking and gambling are rife. As racial tensions spill over causing a trail of violence, bloodshed and murder, Bluey is forced to face the most difficult choices of his life.

'The novel was an enjoyable summer read, well written and researched.' Adam Hussey, Historical Novel Society

Available: Amazon, Apple, Kobo in print and ebook versions